When The Light Turns Dead

Jessica Browner

Published by Trellis Publishing, 2021.

This is a work of fiction. Similarities to real people, places, or events are entirely coincidental.

WHEN THE LIGHT TURNS DEAD

First edition. July 8, 2021.

Copyright © 2021 Jessica Browner.

ISBN: 979-8224970100

Written by Jessica Browner.

WHEN THE LIGHT TURNS DEAD

JESSICA BROWNER

Rain drummed and thrummed on the windshield. *Swish, squeak. Swish, squeak. Swish, squeak.* Tess felt herself becoming hypnotized by the metronome of her windshield wipers. She cranked up the AC and took a deep breath, letting her lips vibrate together on the exhale. Her leg ached, dully. It always did when it rained. Beads of water trailed down the glass trying to escape the rhythmic flick of the wipers. Her headlights reflected off of puddles as the road veered to and fro ahead of her. Wraiths of fog twisted and coiled their wispy fingers, beckoning her further. Trees rose up from the mountainsides like dark sentinels watching her as she passed. Tess looked in her rearview mirror. The faded, yellow highway marks trailed behind her and disappeared into the night.

Her phone beeped, signaling the battery was almost dead. "Shit," Tess felt around in the pile of fast food wrappers in the passenger seat trying to find her car charger. Shadows shrouded everything. The GPS displayed on her phone's screen dimmed to conserve power. She felt around blindly, glancing from the rain soaked road to the shadow-veiled seat beside her. "Ugh!" Tess frustratedly jabbed her finger into the button for the overhead light to come on and squinted as it blinded her momentarily. Through the slits of her eyes, she saw the charger sprawled in the floorboard between empty coffee cups and candy wrappers. Tess looked from the road back to the charger. Her phone beeped again. With an irritated groan, she leaned towards the passenger seat and extended her hand downwards. She shifted her eyes back to the road once more before reaching further for the cord. Tess's fingers barely grazed against the cable. She sighed and tossed an aggravated glance at her hand. *Almost...almost....gotcha!* Tess pulled herself back up into a sitting position. The phone charger was grasped triumphantly in her right hand. She smiled, pleased with herself, but her smile only lasted a second. Tess's car slammed into the bumper of a vehicle that had been parked in the road with its lights off. There wasn't enough time to swerve. There wasn't even enough time to scream.

Tess woke up to smoke rising from her airbag. Glass tinkled out of her hair as she raised her head. She blinked. Her neck was already bruised from where the seatbelt had been during the impact. She moved her neck gingerly. Her fingers fumbled as she tried to undo her safety restraint. Rain pelted against her exposed dashboard. The windshield was busted out, and the hood was crumpled. Shards of glass were tossed carelessly in the floorboard and across the highway. Tess struggled to open her door. The frame had been bent causing the door to wedge shut. The metal groaned as she forced it away from the warped door frame.

Chunks of glass spilled onto the road as she pulled herself out of the wreckage. The engine had plummeted to the ground upon impact. Her car was totaled. The vehicle in front of her had a busted fender, and the back axis was twisted away from the frame. Tess stumbled to the front driver's side door. A knot had started to form on her leg. The other car's front door was already flung open as she peered inside. Something warm slid down her face. She lifted her fingers to brush it away, and they came away sticky with half-dried blood. Tess leaned down to look at herself in the side mirror of the car she had hit. There was a gash and some swelling over her right eye. She touched the skin around her eyebrow gingerly. The cut stung as she kneaded it with her fingertips. Rain drenched her as she examined at her reflection.

Tess turned back to face the deserted car. How long had it been sitting here? She splashed across the pavement back to her own heap of junk. Her hair was plastered to the sides of her face as she searched through the trash in the floorboards for her phone. Wrappers and soda cans clanked and rustled as she rifled through them. She paused as she heard a faint beeping noise. Tess looked around for the source of the sound. She sloshed to the other side of her car and waited a moment. *Beep, beep.* Tess trudged away from her car to the right-hand side of the road. *Beep, beep.* Rain bounced off of the asphalt and splattered onto the grass. She knelt down and rummaged through a pile of damp, fallen leaves.

The screen of her phone was cracked into a spider web pattern. Tess picked it up and ran her thumb across the display. Chipped edges grabbed at her skin, but it lit up faintly in response to her touch. She typed in her passcode and pulled up the dial pad. She dialed 991 and heard a busy tone. She hung up and dialed again. Still busy. She pulled the phone away from her ear and stared at it for a second. "Oh my gosh. I'm such an idiot." Tess said under her breath as she punched in 911 with trembling fingers.

"911, what's your emergency?" A young woman answered the line.

"Hi, yes, I've been in a car accident," Tess paused waiting for a response. She gently probed the contusion on her shoulder, "Hello?" Silence. She pulled the phone away again and looked at the black screen. Tess held down the power button. Her phone flashed for a second and then went black again. Dead.

The last town had been about thirty minutes back. Tess kicked the front tire of her car in frustration. Shooting pains radiated from her foot to her shin. Tess sucked in a sharp breath as the pain took her off guard. She leaned her head against the warped, metal frame and shook her head from side to side allowing it to come to rest facing the way she had been headed. A flash of lightening illuminated the mountainside. In the distance, she saw a figure through the sheets of rain pulling something into the woods. "Hey!" Tess yelled and waved her arms, but her voice was drowned out by a cacophonous crack of thunder. The figure heaved and tugged, struggling to get past the tree line.

Lightening carved its way through the darkness again, and Tess focused on the shapes. Her heart skipped a beat. The figure was a man, hunched over with an unnatural gait. He was pulling a woman behind him. He paused suspiciously for a moment to make sure no one saw them before hobbling off again. The woman's head bounced limply against her chest as he jolted through the rain, dragging her into the darkness of the forest. Tess instinctively crouched behind her car as the next crash of thunder rattled through her. Rain drops pinged against the warped metal behind her. Her heart pounded against her ribs. No phone. She couldn't call for help. If he took that woman into the woods, there was a good chance she would never be found again. Tess pressed her hand to her chest. The metal plates of her dog tags under her shirt dug into her skin. *Shit.* Tess rolled her eyes and shook her head. She had to go after them.

Still crouched, she moved up beside the parked car she had hit and peered around its front bumper. Her head throbbed with each heartbeat. Tess scanned the edge of the woods. No sign of them. She ran to the nearest tree on the left-hand side of the road where the two figures had disappeared. Lightening contorted the shadows around her as she peered between the tree trunks. After a few paces into the forest, she saw the pair again. She watched as the man slogged through the underbrush, towing the woman behind him. The weight of her body slowed his efforts, but he lugged her along over fallen branches and protruding rocks. Twigs cracked under her weight and leaves rustled in her wake. From this distance, Tess couldn't tell if the woman was dead or alive.

The man stopped for a moment, as if he could feel Tess's eyes boring into him. Tess ducked back behind the tree, pressing her back flat against the rough bark. She squeezed her eyes shut. Rain dripped from her bangs along the curve of her nose as she strained to hear more than just the roar of her own pulse. Blood pounded in her ears. Her lungs seized as she held her breath. Wind sliced through the skeleton trees. Tess gasped as the chill curdled her blood and made her skin prickle into tiny bumps. Her eyes flew open with panic as her trembling hand stifled her gasp and clutched at her mouth. Tess's eyes darted back and forth, praying he hadn't heard her. Her other hand pressed harder into the bark of the tree. Her finger tips wedged into the grooves, white and bloodless from the force.

Leaves started to rustle again. Tess waited, listening. Her heart spasmed with fear. Slowly, the sound trailed farther away. She leaned her head to the side and peeked around the trunk. Tess could see his back retreating further into the woods. The woman stirred. He turned towards his hostage and hit her in the back of the head with something. From this far away Tess couldn't tell what it was, but the woman went limp again. He adjusted his grip on her arms and started pulling her deeper into the darkness.

Tess waited for the next rumble of thunder before she moved to another tree. She used the harshness of the storm to hide her progression as she followed the man. She looked over her shoulder. She couldn't see the road anymore. The path back to her car was concealed in a tangle of branches. Mud gave way beneath the carpet of dead leaves. She caught herself on a fallen branch and regained her footing. Twigs pulled at her matted, wet hair and snagged on her clothing. She couldn't see the man anymore. He and his hostage had disappeared behind a thicket of brambles up ahead. Droplets of rain splattered against the coating of leaves on the forest floor and trickled down the bark of the trees. Tess eased up to the tangle of thorns where she had last seen the man and woman. Light reflected off of the dead, wet leaves. She glanced around the twisted vines as the light scattered, obscured for a moment.

Hidden behind the thorned mesh was a weather-worn cabin. The windows were cloudy with specks of dirt and nicotine stains. Smoke rose unsteadily from a cockeyed chimney. The thatched roof sagged and bristled. The knotted wood was split and splintered on the ends. Inside the cabin, a shadow passed in front of the window. Tess quickly ducked back. She slowed her breath as she peered around again. She could see a layer of concrete with a rusted door sunk into the ground near the cabin.

Tess hunkered down and eased herself forward in a crouch. As she inched closer to the wooden sides of the house, she heard a noise coming from the rust-coated shelter. Tess's heart throttled inside of her. Her breath only came in quick, shallow puffs. Adrenaline spread through her, dimming the pain in her shoulder and the right side of her head. Her leg still ached. She lay herself down in the mud outside of the cellar doors. The grass and leaves had been scrapped away by frequent use. Part of the concrete was chipped off where the door met the cellar's shell.

Tess looked into the gap where the piece of concrete was missing. It took her eyes a moment to adjust to the darkness. At first, all she could see were hunched shadows. Inside, figures moved about. Tess could hear the tinkling of metal and soft sobs. The silhouettes slowly became distinguishable. She could see bits of wrinkled clothing, a cascade of hair over slender shoulders, the slight sheen of metal cuffs as they clanked against the floor. The hairs on the back of her neck stood on end. From her vantage point, Tess couldn't tell how many women were locked in the cellar. She had to get help.

Tess propped herself back up on her hands and knees and scurried away from the peephole. Her legs bumped into something solid as she retreated. Tess's breath caught in her throat. She looked behind her and saw muddy boots. The man was silhouetted against a flash of lightening. Tess flipped over and slid herself away from the abductor in front of her using her palms and heels to shove herself backwards through the mud. The man was bent over. His right shoulder jutted out at an awkward angle causing his body to tilt. His face was scarred with fingernail scratches that were too deep to heal completely. The scars shone eerily in the flickering light from the window. Tess's lower back slammed into the cellar as she tried to back away from him. She heard a whimper from inside. The man raised a slab of wood in his left hand. Tess threw up her arms to shield her head as he swung the two by four towards her. The first blow knocked her face down into the mud. She coughed and gagged as muddy water filled her mouth and lungs, unable to pull herself up. The grit of dirt ground against her teeth as they cracked together. The second blow knocked her unconscious.

Tess found herself riding in a Humvee. It was sweltering outside. Her sand-crusted helmet bounced off of the passenger side window. She looked around her. Benson and Greaves were in the back. Patch was driving like always. They were leading the unit into hostile territory. In the back of her mind, she knew something wasn't right. The sun was too bright. The colors were bleached from her surroundings. Everything looked off. They bounced through potholes while static crunched through the radio com. Her instincts screamed at her that something horrible was about to happen. That was when Patch hit the landmine. Time slowed to a crawl as the vehicle was thrown to its side. She saw Patch's helmet sling off of his head. Benson's body had been thrown from the Humvee on impact. Through the smoke she could see him screaming, clutching his gut. Everything was silent around her. Greaves struggled to free himself from under the wreckage. Someone shifted something off of her. The pressure was replaced by intense pain. The world was hazy. Tess was pulled from the vehicle. A chunk of shrapnel was sticking out of her leg. All she could feel was the pain. The pain drowned out the smell of burning flesh, the sounds of men dying, the words of the medic standing over her. The pain was the only thing that existed.

Tess gasped as she came to. Her body jerked away from cold darkness that surrounded her. Shackles held her arms close to the damp walls. The smell of unwashed bodies and human excrement strangled her. Stomach acid burned her throat as she retched between her legs—half from the nightmare, half from the stench surrounding her. Her shoes were missing, and the ground was rough against her bare feet. Her leg ached. Nightmares of the crash always made it hurt worse. It was like her body relived part of the trauma each time it happened. She could feel her lip swelling and the metallic taste of blood stained her tongue. A chunk of her cheek was missing where her teeth had gouged into the soft flesh. Tess spit out some blood and the remaining traces of vomit. She squinted into the darkness. Water sprayed from her hair as she tried to shake her bangs out of her eyes. She could hear others in the darkness with her. Muffled sobs were being chocked back. Chains rattled against the walls. All of the women looked to be in their mid-twenties.

"Where are we?" Tess whispered to the bent figure chained closest to her.

"Shh!" Another woman hissed from the wall perpendicular to where Tess was chained. "If he hears you, you'll be next." Her voice quavered. She glanced at the wall opposite from her. Tess followed her gaze. She could make out the shadows of steps leading up to a wooden door. There was no handle.

"What does he do?" Tess strained against her chains and leaned towards the woman who had spoken. Tess could see thin lines etched into the walls. The lines started two thirds of the way up each of the walls and carved their way down to about the shoulders of the seated captives. The other woman shook her head and rocked with her knees pulled up to her chest. Her red hair splayed over her shoulders. "What does he do?" Tess's voice was more forceful the second time she asked.

"Be quiet!" The other woman whispered pleadingly. Her lips trembled and her eyes were dilated with fear.

Floorboards creaked behind the door. Heavy, uneven footsteps grew louder as they thumped against the wooden planks. All of the women recoiled from the sound. The woman who had spoken to Tess began to shake uncontrollably. On the other side of the door, metal scraped against metal. The sound was like nails on a chalkboard. It ground into Tess's bones as she tried to cover her ears.

The door busted open. The disfigured form of the man that Tess had followed into the woods was framed against the light coming from inside the house. His silhouette was jaggedly grotesque. "Eenie, meanie, miney, mo." the man's voice grumbled as he talked, "Pick a bitch and gut her slow." He had a knife in his hands moving it from side to side with each word. "If she hollars, cut her throat. Eenie, meanie, miney, mo." The tip of his blade pointed to the woman that had hushed Tess.

"No, no, please," the woman begged. Her body crumpled as low to the ground as it could, trying to shrink away from him. "Please, please." She cried as she begged him not to take her. "Oh, God, no." Her sobs descended into unintelligible, animalistic noises as he approached her.

Tess watched as he loomed over them. The man's twisted shadow fell over the pleading woman in front of him. He drug the tip of his roughhewn knife into the cellar wall behind her, slowly making his way down the cement until it was directly above her head. As he scraped the metal along the rock, tiny bits of cement dust fell on top of her heaving body. The knife left a shallow, grizzled path carved behind it, adding one more etching to the wall.

He stuck the tip of the blade under her chin and tilted it up until she was looking directly at him. Most of the other women had turned their heads away. Only Tess and a dark haired girl kept their eyes on the scene unfolding in front of them. Tess felt herself drawn to the terror in front of her. She couldn't make herself look away. The red headed woman's eyes squeezed shut and her lips shook. Their captor turned the blade so that it was pointed at her jugular vein while he pulled a small key out of the left pocket of his pants. The man unlocked the heavy cuffs around his victim's wrists as he applied more pressure with the blade. When both of her wrists were free, he shoved the key back into his pocket and grabbed a handful of her matted, red hair.

He jerked the woman to her feet. He wrenched her up by her hair up so that she had to stand on her tip toes to keep from having strands ripped out of her scalp. Silent tears fell down her cheeks. Her knees threatened to buckle under her as he forced her towards the door, knife still at her throat. Tess saw the blood drain out of her face with every step. The woman stumbled up the stairs, and the door slammed shut behind them. Tess could hear a bolt slide into place on the other side as the door was secured in place.

Tess's heart raced as she strained to hear what was happening behind the closed door. She expected a scream or some sound of altercation, but there was nothing. No thump, no shriek, no sound at all. After about fifteen minutes, Tess began to smell something. It was familiar and sickening. It was a smell she would never be able to forget—a smell that still haunted her. It was the smell of burning flesh.

After what felt like an hour, the bolt on the other side of the door slid free. The man came back into the cellar. He had a platter of meat in his hands. He tossed chunks of seared flesh to the women like a man tossing scraps to his dogs. He scoffed at them with a snort and then made his way back into the house. Some of the women kicked the meat away, choosing to go hungry. One of them—the dark haired girl who had watched with Tess as the redhead was taken—looked at the meat and then over to the empty shackles where the other woman had been. She picked up the meat in front of her. Her hands shook as she pulled a strand of long, red hair off of the cooked flesh. Her cheeks were sunken, and Tess could see the delicate bones of her fingers and wrists through her taut skin. The woman closed her eyes as she lifted the meat to her mouth and sank her teeth into it. She chewed slowly at first, but the more she ate, the more fervently she tore into it. Bits of fat clung to her lips and cheeks.

After the woman finished eating she looked down at her hands, disgusted with herself. She wiped the grease from her fingers onto her tattered clothing. She avoided Tess's gaze and curled into herself. The other women were trying to sleep in awkward positions. Their chains kept them from finding much comfort. Tess struggled as her own eyes became heavy. The events of the day threatened to overwhelm her. Her body needed sleep. She couldn't think clearly anymore.

Tess found herself on a mock search and rescue mission. One of her men had been taken by Alpha Two. Tess positioned herself outside of the main training zone, facing the tent where the objective was held captive. She used the underbrush as cover as she scouted the area. She signaled for two of her men to veer right and draw fire. They ran and took cover behind a stack of wooden crates. They were armed with paintball guns to simulate fire. While the Alpha team was focused on the decoys, Tess steadied her weapon, waiting for the most opportune moment. Her men took out two of the enemies. One of the men inside the tent peeked through the opening. Tess lined up her shot. Before she could pull the trigger, a sharp pain erupted between her shoulder blades. She punched the ground with her fist. Damnit! She rolled over to see Alpha Two's commander standing over her. "Hesitation gets you killed." He smirked as he held out his hand to help her up.

Tess woke up, drenched in a cold sweat. She looked around her trying to shake away the haze of sleep. She had to do something. He was right. Hesitation was going to get her killed. Tess examined the metal cuffs on her wrist. They were a steel semicircle with a bar guarding the opening of the circle. The sweat on her wrists added a small amount of lubrication. She pulled her thumb in towards her palm, making her hand as small as possible. Tess pulled with all her strength. The metal gouged into her skin and scraped as she forced her hand to collapse into itself. One cuff clattered to the floor. The sound woke a few of the other captives who stirred and looked at her. Her knuckles bled where the skin had been rubbed off. Slivers of her skin clung to the steel. Tess opened and closed her fist. No structural damage. The woman who had eaten the flesh earlier sat up, watching intently. Tess used her free hand to grasp at the other cuff. She held the shackle with her free hand as she twisted her other hand free. Tess rubbed her wrists and pulled herself up onto her knees. She crawled over to the woman who had eaten the meat and started trying to help her get free.

The dark haired woman waited until Tess was less than an arm's length away. She looped the chain of her cuffs over Tess's throat and pulled, tightening the links into a metal noose. The woman started screaming as loud as she could. Tess struggled and fought to get her fingers between the chain and her neck. She drove her elbow into the dark haired woman's ribs. The bones gave way with a satisfying crack. The woman's scream ceased in a gasp. One of the broken ribs had pierced her lung. The woman's grip faltered, and Tess untangled herself from the metal.

The door burst open, and their captor charged in. His knife was clutched in his hand as he looked from Tess to the injured woman. He growled at Tess and charged. Tess dodged his attack, scrambling away. The man sliced at the air. Tess jumped behind him and drove a kick into the back of his knee, knocking him off balance as he stumbled and crashed into the floor. Tess connected with is kidney and liver as she pounded his lower back with punches. Her bleeding knuckles cried out in pain with every impact. She gritted her teeth.

The man swung his arm back, and his elbow collided with Tess's temple. She fell to the cold floor. Her vision was blotted with dark, pulsating spots. Everything rippled and waved. She saw the man get to his feet. Her gaze grew dark around the edges. The blackness slowly encroached and filled her full field of vision. The last thing Tess saw was the man's boot coming towards her face as he reared back and kicked her in the head.

"Miss Finch, I cannot help you unless you are willing to help yourself." Tess was laying down on a couch in her shrink's office. Everything was black and white. "I really think you should consider this opportunity." He handed her a brochure for a PTSD support group. The front cover had a picture of a mountain lodge on it.

"We done here?" Tess stood up and shoved the brochure in her back pocket. She left before he had a chance to say anything. When she stepped through the door, the world shifted.

Tess was standing in a hallway. She saw her mom crying at the dining room table with a half drained bottle of vodka in front of her, "I don't know how to talk to her anymore. Since she came back, she's just not the same." Everything melted away. Tess was outside now. She shoved her bags into her car and punched the lodge's address into her phone's GPS.

Her mom was standing on the porch watching her load the car. Suddenly everything went black, and all she could hear was Patch's voice yelling at her to wake up.

The smell of antiseptic shocked Tess out of her dream. In front of her, laying on a roughly carved wooden table was the woman who had tried to strangle her. A fire flickered in the corner fireplace. Antlers and picture frames hung on the walls. Thick, gritty rope bit into Tess's wrists. She was tied to a wooden chair. The man was applying some type of salve to the dark haired woman's scrapes. Between each of her ragged breaths, he dabbed the frothy blood that bubbled out her mouth with a rag.

The pictures on the wall were of the man in front of her and a little girl. Tess could see the girl's life in the photos. She glanced from birthday pictures to middle school science fairs to high school proms. The pictures stopped after high school. Tess's eyes grew wide as she recognized the girl in the pictures. If you added a few years and subtracted a few pounds, she was the spitting image of the woman on the table.

"She's your daughter?" Tess whispered as she looked at the pictures. The man growled like a beast as he whirled around and faced Tess as she spoke. "How could you lock up your own daughter like that?"

"She was going to leave me. Wanted to go to college." He faced his daughter again. "I would have been alone." His voice sounded like gravel in a blender.

"So you locked her up?" Tess was appalled.

"She was the one good thing I had in my life. I couldn't let her leave." The man pounded his fist on the table, "The world is a horrible place. She needed protection. It was for her own good. When she was lonely, I brought her friends." He gestured to the cellar. "When she was hungry, I fed her. Everything I did was for her." He stroked the woman's cheek as she wheezed. Tess could hear the sincerity in his voice. "She's dying because of you." He looked over his deformed shoulder at Tess.

His fingernails scrapped along the edge of the table. The dying woman raised her hand and touched his face. Tess could see that even after all of twisted things her father had done to her, this woman still loved him. His voice softened at her touch. "Eenie, meanie, miney, mo. Stay with me, it's not time to go." He pleaded with the dark haired girl who managed a small smile before her hand fell back to the table and the light drained out of her eyes.

Tess tried to wiggle her hands free from their bondage, but the rope was so tight that her fingers were already tinged purple. The man watched as his daughter breathed her last breath. He roared in anger and slammed his fist into the nearest wall. Rage devoured him. His eyes were crazed as he spun back to face Tess. He glared at her, anger building, and then marched to the fire. He took an iron poker that was propped against the hearth and plunged it into the heart of the flames. He stumbled out of Tess's field of vision into another room. She could hear him throwing furniture into walls as his grief consumed him.

Her mind was racing. She couldn't feel her fingers anymore. Tess looked around for anything that could help her escape. In that instant, she remembered another search and rescue mission when her team had held another soldier hostage. He had broken the chair they had tied him to in order to free himself. Tess rocked back and forth until her bare feet landed on the planks of the floor. She leaned forward and then threw herself backwards as hard as she could. The velocity of her force propelled her towards the ground. The back of the chair landed on the hard, wood floor, shattering the chair underneath her. The arms of the chairs were still held in place against her forearms by the rope.

Before she could undo the knots, the sound of shattering wood brought the man back into the room. He saw Tess on the ground. Wrath contorted his face as he grabbed the white-hot poker and charged at her. Tess struggled to her feet. She dodged as he jabbed the heated metal towards her chest. Tess crossed behind him as he over stretched on his attack. She leapt onto his back and locked her forearms around his throat, cutting off his oxygen supply. He spun around and slammed his back into the wall, knocking the wind out of her. She lost her death grip around his neck. Tess cried out as she grabbed one of the wooden planks still strapped to her arms and thrust the splintered edge into the man's throat.

He fell to his knees, clutching his neck. Tess forced the wood deeper into his throat. It gave way a little as the splinters pushed through his larynx. Blood spurted from his severed arteries, coating Tess's arms. The man swayed slightly as he bled out and lost consciousness before falling forward. Tess slid off of his back and rolled him over. She used her trembling, free hand to untie the rope that secured her arm to the plank protruding from the dead man's neck. Once that arm was free, she tugged on the other rope with her fingers and teeth until it released its grip. Feeling started slowly returning to her fingertips. After her arms were loose, she started searching his pockets until she found the key to the shackles.

Tess held the tiny key between her slippery fingers. She leaned back and braced herself against the wall, taking a few deep breaths. Blood soaked into her pants as she sat there. She brushed a strand of hair out of her face, leaving behind a streak of blood on her forehead. Tess pulled herself up out of the sticky, red puddle and stumbled to the door that led down to the cellar.

The other women watched as she walked down the stairs. They flinched away from her at first. Her bare feet left fresh, red footprints in her wake. Tess unlocked the other captives one by one. They huddled together, still not fully believing they were going to escape. Together, they climbed up the stairs into the shack. The women walked past the bloody body of their captor and out into the forest clearing. The sky was a pale grey-blue tinged with pink and apricot. The sun was coming up. It took a few minutes for their eyes to adjust to the light after being underground for so long. They breathed in the air, free of the smell of their own filth.

Tess led them through the trees back to the highway. Everything looked different in the daytime. The trees were less menacing. Twigs and small rocks jabbed into the soles of her bare feet as they walked. Tess's adrenaline was wearing off. Her injuries started to ache and throb. The pain was getting harder to ignore. After some time, the sounds of cars zooming past grew from a faint hum into a roar. The women looked around as they stepped onto the faded asphalt. A few hundred yards down the road to the right, Tess saw the wreckage of her car. A few police cruisers were parked on either side of collision while officers examined the scene. Tess led her bedraggled group towards the policemen. Her feet scraped along the highway.

"I think that's my car." One of the women said softly as she squinted in the light. Tess glanced at her. She must have been the woman Tess saw the man dragging into the woods.

When the officers caught sight of the disheveled women, they ran to meet them. One of the policemen radioed for back up and several ambulances. "Is anyone hurt? What happened?"

Tess explained everything that had gone on in the worn down cabin. Ambulances came and medics wrapped the women in blankets while policemen took their statements. A team of officers was deployed into the woods to examine the location of the tragedy. The women were taken to the local hospital, and their loved ones were called. Some newspapers told the story of a mentally unstable man torturing women for pleasure. Some told the story of a family man who simply got carried away trying to protect his daughter. Tess seemed to be the only one to realize that when it came to human beings, circumstances were never really black and white. The truth was a just jumbled shade of grey.

THE CULTIES

MARTIN LONG

'The cult?' asked the shopkeeper, his small, watery eyes moving behind thick spectacles as he thought, 'Oh! You mean the Process lot outside of town, yeah?'

'That's the one mister Jones, can you tell us what you know?' Jen asked, training her camera on him, trying to ignore his nervous glances into the lens.

'Well, not much to tell really.' began Jones, looking wistfully out of the shop window, 'They turned up, oh must've been the 60's I think, I was only a kid then, I remember seeing 'em in the store with my ma. Weird lot, all wore suits, even the kids hah! Funny story about that actually, there was a time...'

Jen stifled a sigh as the older man launched into another meandering and ultimately pointless account of something that had happened to him in previous years. She kept the camera on him, sitting steady on its small tripod, but found her mind wandering. Investigating the Process Church had seemed like such a brilliant idea when she had first thought of it. The cult of Devil worshipers who, rumor had it, performed satanic rituals and sacrificed children on altars. Jen didn't have much time for all that, but what was interesting was their links to various grisly unsolved murders and the cases of Charles Manson and the Son of Sam killer. There were rumors that both men were either members of, or had contact with the cult, and were directed to kill by them. As for the unsolved murders, the cult had been accused publicly at least once that she could find, but the case was settled out of court and the rest were officially cold cases due to "lack of evidence". The Church had even taken to the TV waves after this court case to denounce its accusers.

It had all seemed just that little bit too much like there was something hiding in the dark underbelly of the Church to Jen, and once she'd caught the scent, she couldn't get it out of her mind. Portland had seemed suddenly dull and uncomplicated, the potential documentary stories there mostly on why, like, weed is totally the best maaan. Her mind kept jumping to the articles she had read, the forum posts that had insinuated the behind-the-scenes goings on of the Church were even worse than they knew. It had been too much, and she knew herself too well to think that there was any point in fighting it. So here she was, in the ironically named town of Devil's Lake, population 7,141. It was much like many other North Dakotan small towns she had seen - flat, isolated and spread out far further than its population would have one believe. Much like other small towns she had seen also, there was a strong trend towards alcoholism and drug abuse as well as an underlying sensation that the desolation of the badlands had somehow crept, insidiously, into the air of the place. On the drive in she had found herself hypnotized and unnerved by the sheer size of the overcast, October, gray sky and the damp, straw colored plains that stretched to the horizon in every direction. Jen could see herself becoming lost in the endless flats, with no features to guide herself by either by land or sky, wandering, slowly being consumed by the desolation. Despite the ridiculousness of the image, it had set in motion an uneasy sensation deep in her mind that was yet to settle. It was this sensation that had probably given her the nightmares the night before and had influenced her decision to buy wine to make sure she slept soundly that night. The fact that the man behind the counter in the shop to get said wine was happy to talk to her was something of an aside, if she was honest. Still, it'd made for useful B-roll if nothing else.

'...we just thought he was stupid because obviously, we knew they weren't doin' no rituals or anything down there!'

As if thinking about him had tuned her brain back into his voice, Jen realized that he was saying something worth paying attention to.

'I'm sorry mister Jones-'

'Just call me Bob, everyone else around here does! Well, those that don't go to that damned Kmart...' his expression showed what he thought of those types.

'Bob then,' continued Jen, 'I'm sorry, just a slight hiccup with the camera here, didn't get that last part, could you repeat it for me please? You're doing really well, are you sure you've not been on TV before?' she flashed him a smile and casually flicked her blonde hair behind her ear, a one-two punch of charm that rarely failed to convince. Using technological failure just enhanced the effect, it had an air of "Computers eh? What ya gonna do?" that everyone could connect with. Her charm seemed to have the desired effect as Jones blushed a little, and began to repeat his story.

'Well, I was just sayin' that back when I was a kid, a friend of mine, Randy, said that he saw some kind of ritual goin' on in the basement of the Church, Devil Worship or something. He swears up and down to this day he saw them all chanting and swaying around some kind of altar, all dressed up in these big black robes.'

Jen felt a prickle somewhere in the back of her brain, this was gold. It set up the continuation of the mystery perfectly.

'Obviously,' Bob continued, 'We all thought he was just making it up, we were only about twelve at the time, and God how we would make up all kinds of stories.'

'And was he?'

'Hah! Well, there's the question ain't it? It'd be exciting if he wasn't wouldn't it? Like a horror movie!'

'Yes I suppose it would be... ' said Jen, slowly, surprised. She'd expected hostility to the Church certainly - that she could work with - but this kind of casual dismissiveness, that didn't make for a particularly exciting narrative now did it? She decided to follow the lead anyway, leave no stone unturned and all that.

'Bob, you wouldn't happen to still be in contact with your friend, would you? It would be great if we could hear this story from him ourselves.' she asked, the smile returning.

'Who Randy? Won't be hard to get a hold of him, he lives just at the other end of town.' Bob chuckled to himself as though this was somehow hilarious. Jen sighed inwardly, she hated small towns. 'Hang on,' continued Bob, when he had controlled himself, 'I'll write down the address for you.' He busied himself with a pen, and Jen stopped recording, feeling she had enough.

The shop bell suddenly rang and they turned to see a young man in a police uniform enter; Jen couldn't help but notice he was incredibly good looking, strong jaw, fine boned cheeks, bright blue eyes and an easy smile. He must have been the apple of many a Devil's Lake girl's eyes.

'What's all this then?' he asked cheerily as he spotted the camera and microphone.

'Mornin' Thomas,' said Bob, returning the deputy's smile, 'This fine young lady here is making a movie about the Process lot, were asking me some questions.'

'Well, I hope they didn't listen to a word you said.' he turned to Jen conspiratorially, 'He's not to be trusted!' he whispered with a wink.

Jen laughed,

'I'm Jen,' she said, extending her hand, enjoying the firm, but also somehow delicate handshake she received.

'Pleased to meet you, I'm Thomas, Deputy of Devil's Lake.' he said, smiling broadly, 'Investigating our resident cult eh?'

'That's the plan anyways.'

'Well, I hope you find something good because, between you and me, they might seem weird, but don't go listening to the stories you'll hear from these hicks' he waved a hand towards Bob, who raised a middle finger good-naturedly in return. 'Those Church folk are duller than week old dishwater, least as far as I know.'

'And what about what you don't know?' Jen asked, her smile becoming shark-like, sensing an opportunity, 'What about the links to Charles Manson and the Son of Sam killings?'

'Well, I don't know about all that,' Thomas replied, shrugging, 'but if you want to run around town chasing ghost stories and conspiracy theories, all I'll say is better you than me.' he smiled in a way that said he thought she was wasting her time, but in it Jen thought she saw a hint of flirtatious challenge there too.

'So you don't think there's anything worth my time here?' she asked, mirroring his smile.

'Honestly? Unless you want to keep that camera pointed at this beautiful face all day', he preened jokingly, 'I'd say you're fresh out of luck.'

'Well, I'll bear that in mind, Deputy, but as I'm here now,' she reached over the counter to pick up the address Bob had written down, 'I might as well keep going, right?'

'Right.'

*

Randy's place was on the outskirts of town, past an old industrial yard. The rusting hulks of old machinery sticking up into the air seemed like the decaying bones of a once massive animal, now dead and forgotten. For some reason the image made Jen shiver, and she turned the heat up in the car as she drove past. Despite it being almost midday, the day hadn't got any brighter, and the lowering clouds sat heavy and uniform over the landscape. In town, it was easy to forget the sense of being somewhere abandoned, worn down and worn out, but further out it returned with force. There was a feeling, like a background hum, here that set her teeth on edge, made her hackles rise. She pulled up outside a run-down, one-story wooden house with peeling white paint and a garden in desperate need of tending. The neighborhood wasn't much better, all cracked tarmac, rusting decades-old cars and skinny children playing on hand-me-down bikes. Jen felt the background buzz rise again in her head but put it aside as she reached for her camera to take some initial B-roll, focusing her lens on the worst aspects of the decaying area.

'Right Jennifer, let's do this.' she took a deep breath and stepped out of the car.

Randy, when he answered the door, was a tall, slim man of similar ages to Bob, balding and with the nicotine stained teeth of someone whose lungs are more used to smoke than air. Taciturn at first, he quickly changed his tune when he realized he had a chance to be "on TV". Inside, his house was classic 70s pre-fab, all brown lino and felt-feel sofas with more stains than color. The air was dusty and thick with the smell of stale smoke and dog, although she couldn't see any evidence a dog lived there. She decided to set up in his dingy living room, the lighting being the best, and the smell the least. The tar staining on the walls looking like a flood water line and in one corner sat a trophy cabinet thick with dust, the glass greasy and opaque, with rows of gleaming gold awards sitting, seemingly forgotten, within.

'What did you win the medals for?' asked Jen as she set up the tripod, trying to get a feel for what type of interview subject Randy was going to be.

'Oh them?' he asked, puffing out his chest proudly, 'Got them for baseball, I was the best Junior League batter in the town, coulda gone Pro.'

'Very impressive. What stopped you going Pro then, Randy, do you mind if I call you Randy?'

He waved her question away, and his hand came up to his right shoulder.

'Busted my shoulder during a game. Swung so hard the bat broke, but doctors said I tore all the muscles in there something awful, wouldn't ever be able to hit the same again. And wouldn't you know it, they were right...'

He gazed off into the middle distance, his mind clearly back to that day he discovered his dreams were dead around him. Jen made to comfort him, then thought better of it - anything she could say would just sound trite.

There was an awkward pause.

'So, Randy,' she began, trying to break the moment, 'Like I said at the door, your friend Bob tells me that you have an interesting story about the Process Church, would you mind sharing it?' Jen moved the camera to take in his face, he eyed it nervously.

'The culties? That was years and years ago... Still, I know what I saw!' his eyes roved her face for signs of disbelief.

'I believe you, I sincerely do,' said Jen, nodding sympathetically, 'I just want to get the story on record, it'll be a vital part of the documentary.'

How true that statement was was anyone's guess, but it paid to nice.

'Well, it was back when me and Bob were kids, must've been about ten at the time. The culties had just moved into town and all us kids were pretty sure they were up to no good. So we did what any good kid would do, we tried to spy on them didn't we? Usually it'd just be us going up to their place, they got a big piece of land just on the outskirts with all these fences and such like, and climbing over the fence to go touch the nearest building or whatever. You know, kid games, thinkin' we were so brave.'

'Did you get caught?'

He laughed, and with a motion of his hands asked if she minded if he smoked.

'It's your house.' Jen responded.

'There were a couple of times.' he continued, lighting a cigarette and taking a couple of long, harsh drags, 'They used to have these big dogs they'd sometimes let out if the townsfolk were giving them any bother. I tell you, you don't know how fast you can run 'till you've got one of those breathing down your neck.'

'Was there a lot of friction between them and the town?'

'Oh some, much as you'd expect, to be honest. This is was during the Cold War 'member, everyone was so paranoid about Ruskies hiding under the bed that they got kind of jumpy.'

'What about now?'

A shrug,

'Don't know. The Church ain't what it used to be, think a lot of the young ones have jumped ship, so to speak. They keep to themselves and everyone ignores them, it seems to work.'

Jen nodded, wondering if she really was, as the deputy said, barking up the wrong tree after all.

'So bring me back to the night of your story, what happened?'

Randy sat back in his seat, suddenly pensive, his eyes distant as he smoked.

'It was a night a lot like the other times we went up there. There was maybe four or five of us, me, Bob, another couple of guys and Sally Treacher... Now at the time, I had a hell of a crush on Sally, so wherever she'd go, I wouldn't be far behind.' he shook his head, smiling at the memory, 'Anyways, we get up to the fence and as usual the daring starts. Bob gets dared to go over the fence and touch the closest house, which he does, then it comes to me.' he finished the cigarette and immediately lit another, 'Now, I've never been the bravest guy around, and when I was a kid that was even more true. So when they start daring me to go break into one of the buildings, I'm not for it. But still, there's Sally, looking all disappointed in me, so I decide to one up the lot of them and say I'll break into the Church, and steal something to prove it.' he paused, flicked ash off the cigarette, eyes distant, 'God kids are so stupid... I got over the fence, had done it before y'see, got into the grounds, and went up to the Church. It's this big old white thing, think it was built about a hundred years ago, all wood. There's some kind of service going on in the Church so I decide to get myself into the basement; my plan was to get in there, get the first thing I could carry and get out.'

'So what happened?' Jen asked, finding herself taken in by Randy's story, despite herself.

'I got in through one of the windows, turns out they didn't lock them back then. The place looked normal enough, a bunch of extra chairs and tables, old furnace, random crap, you know, the usual basement stuff yeah? Well, I find this like model monster I spied on some shelf, must've been for the kids, and I've just put it in my pocket when I hear voices coming from further down.'

'Further down? What do you mean?'

'The voices were like coming from underneath me.'

Jen felt a shiver go through her.

'What happened then?'

'Well I freaked out of course, didn't I? I thought I was going to get caught, so I hid, but after a while, I realize that the voices weren't getting any closer, and there was this weird light coming up from the floor. So I found a hole to look through and...'

He stopped, brow furrowed.

'What did you see.'

'Don't know, to be honest. There was a whole bunch of them standing around this big stone, all in these black robes, and all chanting something I couldn't understand. In the middle was this woman, she was naked and had all these symbols drawn all over her... I think it was blood. She was wearing this skull, I think it was a sheep skull, you know, like a ram? And was dancing and yelling like nothing I've ever seen... Then they brought this kid forward, don't know who she was, and the woman had this big knife and...'

'And?' Jen asked, now on the edge of her seat.

'I don't know, I bolted out of there as fast as I could. I told everyone about it, but no one believed me, and there never was any missing girl, not around here anyways... but I never went back to there, never again...'

He drew hard on the cigarette and stubbed it out violently, as though he was taking his fear out on it.

'Well, thank you for sharing that with us Randy... It's quite a story.' Jen said, finding herself shaken by his tale, despite its apparent fancifulness. 'You wouldn't happen to have the model you stole would you?'

'It's in the trophy case, take it if you want. Don't even know why I kept it to be honest...'

Jen moved over to the case, taking the camera with her. The glass was greasy and opaque, so she had to open it. Behind was rows of baseball medals, tarnished but still proud somehow, and then, at the bottom, in the corner of a shelf on its own, a small figure sat. She picked it up and held it to where the camera could see it. It was about two inches high, and intricately detailed, but it carried with it a heavy sense of revulsion, almost to the point of fear. The creature was monstrous, twisted beyond all belief, its facial features distorted, its mouth caught between a toothy leer and a scream, its limbs tangled and broken.

'I remember my Pa saying to me once,' said Randy, over her shoulder, "The devil ain't so bad son, it's people you got to worry about."

*

That night, after most of a bottle of wine, Jen found herself reviewing the footage of the day in her motel room. The motel was near the center, and, for a small town, was simply but practically furnished. Suspicious stains were at a minimum and there were no cockroaches in the bathroom, so Jen called it a win, as far as she was concerned at least. Scrolling back through the footage, she paused it on Randy's face, its expression pensive and worried as he told his story. It had been a strange start to the investigation. She hadn't expected to find many people willing to talk to her, but at the same time, what they had said wasn't anything particularly useful. Sure, Randy's story would make for a great set up to the mystery in terms of the narrative, but aside from the model, which now sat on her bedside table, leering at her, there was no evidence that anything he'd said was true. The model didn't prove anything, and the story, conveniently, couldn't be backed up by anyone else. Still, she thought, poking a finger at the model, she had some great visuals already. Her gut still told her there was something here aside from local legend and hearsay, something worth finding out. It was a feeling Jen had learned to trust over her career and had lead to more than one award nomination, if not outright win. Still, if she could get into the meat of this one, it could be what she needed to get past that plateau, and... Her gaze fell on the phone that sat, discarded, on the bed beside her, it's alert light blinking at her, telling her of the multiple messages Daniel had left her. A guilty feeling squirmed through her stomach before she quashed it coldly; not now. The documentary first, the rest of her life... later. As if prompted by her discomfort, her phone began to ring. A jolt of panic was quickly replaced with a kind of relieved confusion as a number she didn't know appeared on the caller ID; she thumbed the screen to answer.

'Hello?'

The caller on the other end hung up upon hearing her voice. The wrong number, she guessed.

Through the thin wall behind her, she could hear whoever was in the next room talking on the phone.

'No no, it's fine... How are you?... You need to be careful! How's the treatment going?... I know, but you need to keep fighting okay? I'll be home after this job... I know but we need the money...'

The rest she couldn't make out, but shortly after there was a click of a phone being hung up, and quiet sobbing followed.

She put her headphones in and switched on her favorite playlist, trying to blot out the world that insisted on getting in.

*

Jen sat outside the Process Church compound, watching autumn leaves blow across the courtyard in swirling flurries. Within the high, steel fence there were fifteen or so squat looking buildings, all painted white to match the church that stood proudly in the center. The grass at the sides of the paths was well tended and the trees in the compound gave the place an almost peaceful air. It flew in the face of what she potentially wanted it to look like, but it would have to do.

'Well, no time like the present.' said Jen to herself, scooping up her main camera, and also checking the feed from the button camera she had pinned to her chest. She had learned long ago that when dealing with potentially jumpy subjects, always have another camera ready. People had a bad habit of knocking unwanted cameras to the ground to smash into a hundred, expensive, useless pieces.

She got out of the car and strolled casually across the quiet road to the wrought iron gate that served as the entrance to the compound. As she approached, a tall, burly man who wore a dull gray suit and a kind but insincere smile came out of a small booth to meet her.

'Good morning ma'am, can I help you?' his voice was pleasant and even, no sign of aggression or hostility. Jen had a feeling that could change quickly.

'Good morning!' she replied cheerily, approaching him with her hand outstretched and an open smile, 'Jennifer Mathews, how are you doing today?'

'I'm very well thank you, ma'am.' the guard replied, clasping her hand gently for a moment before letting go. 'How can I help you?'

'Well, I'm here, as you might see from my camera, to film. I'm a documentary filmmaker you see, and I'm looking at the Process Church, how it came to be, what it believes, and how it's been misunderstood by modern media.' throughout her pitch, she tried to smile and keep eye contact. Fake confidence till you make confidence, it always worked.

'Well that's very interesting ma'am, and normally I'd be happy to let you in for a tour but...' the man's face suddenly became colder, 'The Church doesn't take kindly to those who are looking to do hatchet jobs of our reputation, Miss Mathews. We hear you've been asking around town about us, about, what was it "Devil Worship"? And Charles Manson? And here you are, bold as brass, standing here before us asking if we'll let you in? I don't think so, now I'm going to ask you to leave, and if you don't I will be forced to remove you.'

In that moment, Jen thought about arguing with him, but there was something... a coldness in the man's eyes that scared her more than she expected. She forced her smile to return,

'It was worth a shot, wasn't it?' she asked, trying to lighten the mood again.

'No, I don't really think it was. Now I'm going to ask you one more time to leave, and I suggest you do so.' He glared to emphasize his point, and she felt she had probably outstayed her welcome. Turning on her heel she walked back to her car, feeling herself start to shake with the adrenaline come-down.

'Miss Mathews?' came a call behind her, she turned to the guard, 'Just a piece of friendly advice, if you think a group of people are killing people and worshiping the Devil, maybe going around town and asking anyone who'll listen isn't the smartest plan.'

'Is that a threat?' she asked, bluntly.

'No threat ma'am, like I said, just a word of advice.'

Jen didn't wait to hear any more, instead marching away from him, her head held high and her fists balled as though angry when inside her heart was beating against her ribs like a caged animal. Inside the car, she locked the doors and took a deep breath to try to calm herself. It didn't make sense why she was so scared, she'd been in war zones, had had guns pointed at her by known killers, and yet for some reason the guard, this story... it was already eating into her in a way she'd never experienced before. Glancing over to the guard, she saw him in his booth, talking animatedly into his phone, looking up often towards her car; his expression was grim. Jen started the engine and pulled away hurriedly, anxious to get away from his accusing, dangerous stare.

When she reached the hotel room about half an hour later, she was still feeling nervous and jumpy; the journey not having helped. At a stop light, an old woman had ceased her shuffling walk to stare at her through the windshield, her wizened eyes boring uncomfortably into her. Despite the visible fragility of the woman, her stare unsettled Jen; it somehow held an element of powerful threat, as though it were an omen of bad things to come. She had accelerated hard when the light turned green. Then, further along the road, a black car with deep tinted windows had joined the route behind her and had stayed there until she had turned into her motel. Now, sitting in the parking lot of the motel, she couldn't help but feel like there was someone, something, watching her still. It was a prickle on her back, a chill running up her spine, a shadow at the corner of her vision, and Jen could feel it starting to pick away at the ordered reason of her mind.

'Get it together Jennifer.' she said to herself sternly, gripping the car's wheel tight enough to make her knuckles go white, 'It's just some stories and a bad tempered security guard. Everyone around here thinks the Church is just a bunch of harmless freaks, and everyone can't be wrong can they? No, no of course-'

There was a knock on her car window and she screamed loudly in fright, turning to face she-didn't-know-what, only to find the genial, weather-worn face of the woman who owned the motel.

'Oh Jesus Christ... ' Jen breathed as she opened the door. ' You scared the hell out of me.' she said, letting out a long breath/

'I'm sorry dear!' said the woman, an apologetic smile on her face, 'It was an accident I promise, just saw you sitting there in the car and thought I might as well give you your mail, seeing as I was on my way to do that anyways.' the woman's voice was cracked with long usage but had a warmth to it that was instantly comforting.

'Mail?' Jen asked, frowning.

'Someone dropped it off this morning, said I was to give it to you, and well, here I am!'

'Thanks...'

She took the letter, a cheap stationery store envelope with nothing more than "The documentary maker" written in neat, printed letters on the front. Turning it in her hand, Jen tried to see if there were any identifying markings, anything to show who sent it; finding nothing.

'Who was it th...' she stopped her question to the motel owner as she found that the older woman had disappeared as she inspected the letter.

'Nothing for it I guess.' Jen said to herself, ripping open the letter, then regretting it instantly.

'You're in danger' it read, 'Meet me at Katie's bar, 2pm sharp, today. Will explain all.

Make sure you're not followed. The Church is more dangerous than you think.'

*

Katie's Bar turned out to be a small dive near the center of town. Inside it was dark and smelled of stale beer, unwashed bodies and the faint, acrid odor of urine. Jen wrinkled her nose in disgust, trying not to draw attention to herself as she scanned around, looking to see who she was meeting. It being the middle of the day, there weren't many patrons. There were one or two men who looked like truckers sipping beer and watching the football on the grainy TV above the bar and in the row of booths there was a man passed out asleep on the table closest to her. At one of the booths further along, a portly, middle-aged man with large glasses and a thick coat, rose and caught her eye, motioning that she should join him. She sat down opposite him nervously, not helped by his glancing around every few moments, as though trying to catch someone watching.

'You weren't followed were you?' he asked, his voice low and serious.

'No! Well, I don't think so... I don't know...' she trailed off as she realized how out of her depth she was becoming. Still, she still had her button camera recording everything. If asked she would have said it was because of professionalism, but the cynic in her said it was so they had a higher chance of catching whoever might murder her in cold blood in this backwater town.

'That'll have to do... ' he said, shifting closer so they could talk privately.

'So, what did you mean that I'm in danger?' asked Jen, now glancing around as well, finding the man's anxiety infectious.

'I mean that you've already got their attention by snooping around and if you keep on doing it there's a good chance you're going to end up in an unfortunate "road accident" soon.' he said, as though explaining to a child.

'They wouldn't actually kill me just for asking questions, would they? I mean really?' despite her recent experiences, Jen found it hard to believe that the cult would immediately go for the nuclear option. 'And who are you anyway?'

'Just call me Jack, and ten years ago... the Church took my little girl from me.'

'They took her? Like kidnapped?'

'Like, stole from my front yard and later dumped her body in a ditch at the side of the road, all hacked up and covered in satanic writing.' Jack's voice stayed quiet but the emotional intensity behind it was almost too much to face directly, Jen found herself averting her eyes.

'I'm so sorry...' she said, not knowing what else to say.

'Don't be sorry, it's never done me any good, but I do need your help. I know where there's evidence that can expose them, but they're always watching me so I can't do anything about it. You can use it and expose them, then someone will have to do something.'

'Can't you just go to the police?'

He scoffed,

'I've tried, but without the evidence, they just say they can't do anything about it. There's no link between the Church and Maria's disappearance, at least not on the surface.'

'How do you know it was them?' she asked, suddenly suspicious of this intense man who had contacted her out of the blue.

His face darkened, the light suddenly going out of his eyes,

'I was in the house when she was taken. One little scream, that was all she managed, but I heard it... I ran outside and she was gone, and a black van was driving off. I followed them in my car, wanting to see where they went so I could take her back when they stopped... They went into the Church compound, behind those big iron gates.' He took a deep breath and clenched his fists, 'I tried to get the police to do something about it, but when they searched the Church, there was nothing there, no van, no Maria, no evidence at all. Eventually, everyone thought I was just losing it 'cause I couldn't handle losing my girl, my wife left me... but I couldn't let it go, I can't let it go. They need to pay!' he slammed his fist down on the table loudly, making Jen jump.

'It's okay,' she said soothingly, placing her hand on his, trying to placate him, her mind racing, 'Where is this evidence?'

'It's in the Church, in the basement. I spoke to Randy as well, I know if we can get in there, we'll find what we need.' his eyes burned with conviction, and for the first time she saw the fragility of his mental state; unconsciously she took her hands from his.

'One story isn't a lot to go on to break into somewhere... especially if it's somewhere you think is dangerous.' Jen said, folding her arms and wishing now she hadn't come to this meeting.

'What else am I supposed to do? They took my girl, and they got away with it!' his voice seethed with hatred and barely repressed rage.

'I know, and I'm sorry about your daughter, I really am, but I think I'm going to leave now. It was nice to meet you, Jack.' she made to stand, but he caught her hand roughly.

'Look, I know how this all must look to you, I know I seem crazy, hell I probably am, but look it up, look up my daughter, and the other kids that have gone missing too, and the parents that died when they tried to get justice. You'll see I'm telling the truth! When you do, get me at this number.' He let her go to scrawl a cell phone number onto a bar napkin and then shoved it into her hand. 'You'll see, I promise you will.' he said, then, finally, let her go. Jen didn't reply, instead just nodded and stuffed the napkin in her pocket as she hurriedly left the bar.

When she got back to her car, her mind struggling to process what she had just heard, she found that someone had put a leaflet under her wiper. Taking it out, she unfolded it to find a strange, angular symbol printed on it, with no other identifying features. There had been similar posters around town which Jen had assumed were adverts for a local band or something similar, but now, the sense of being observed returned, and she crumpled the poster in her hands, looking around her to see if anyone was watching. No one seemed to be, but she got in and drove off hurriedly, anxious to put the strange encounter with Jack behind her. The rest of the day she spent driving aimlessly around town, with the vague reason of collecting more B-roll footage to cut into the documentary, but in her mind she kept going back to the events of the last couple of days. Even though nothing, really, had happened, she was shaken to her core. There was something about this place, about the gunmetal sky, the flat, desolate emptiness outside of town and the furtive presence of the Process Church in the background, that sat heavily on her back and poked and prodded at her fears. The town had become threatening to her, and gradually she began to feel that it was one creature, hostile, and trying to squash her like she would an irritating bug. Underneath all that, Jen was surprised to find that her curiosity about the Church, the thing that had lead her here in the first place, hadn't been quelled by her fears, and had somehow only had its flame fanned. Jack's story, and his insistence that she research it... it was too enticing not to do anything about, and eventually, she found herself giving in and heading to the local library.

When there, she discovered that Jack's story was either incredibly well researched, or he was telling the truth. Maria Fontinue, ten years old, snatched from her own front yard by suspects unknown in the early nineties only to be found later dismembered and covered in cuts that formed strange symbols. The police's official line was a solo killer, but her father, Jack Fontinue, accused the Process Church of the crime, which they publicly denied, and no evidence had ever been found to back-up the accusation. It was written off as a tragic, but sadly not unheard of, story of a parent looking for someone to blame after a horrific experience, and Jen couldn't help but still feel that she agreed. That was, until, following her curiosity, she began to look into other disappearances. For a town of fewer than ten thousand people, a lot of people went missing. In the seventies, in one year, four people disappeared suddenly into the ether, never to be seen again, and in the following weeks and months, a good number of their parents, relatives or friends either ended up dead or also missing themselves. They were written off as extreme reactions to the grief of their missing family member or loved one, but as Jen looked through the stories, a pattern began to emerge. Every couple of years, someone would drop off the map suddenly, inexplicably, and for the next year, the rate of murders, suicides, and accidental deaths seemed to jump exponentially. The increases, at least locally, seemed to drop off as time went on, but two where nothing happened in Devil's Lake just so happened to coincide with two other incidents. The Manson family killings and the Son of Sam rampage. As she saw the evidence mount, Jen couldn't suppress a shiver. It felt like she was a fly, and had just noticed for the first time the web that she was caught in. The seeming size and reach of the Church's plans were horrific in their scale. What did it all mean? Why kill all these people? What purpose did it serve? Outside the window, dusk was creeping in, and Jen didn't like the idea of driving after dark in town. She printed copies of all the evidence she could and headed back to her hotel.

On the way back she passed Bob's shop, and frowned as she saw it was cordoned off, with police cars sitting outside it as figures in the white overalls of the CSI came and went. A heavy knot formed in her stomach as she pulled up, her need to know what had happened overriding any fear.

'Oh please no...' she whispered.

An officer approached her window and she wound it down to find Thomas, leaning down to talk to her.

'Evening Miss Mathews, good to see you again, I'm sorry it can't be in a better time.' he said, his face stern.

'What happened here?' she asked, watching an EMT shut the doors on an ambulance.

'Bob... Bob was murdered. They cut his goddamn head off.' Thomas' eyes seemed watery, as though he was on the edge of crying and he took a deep breath.

'Oh my God...' Jen breathed, her mind jumping to the warning Jack had given her; it was already happening, they were getting rid of people who talked.

'Things don't seem to be too great in town at the moment Miss Mathews,' said Thomas heavily, 'If I were you I'd let this documentary of yours lie for a little while, just until things settle down. People around here are likely to reach for their guns first and ask questions later.'

'I'll... bear that in mind. Thank you officer, good night.' she said, dazed, her mind running ahead of her as she saw the noose begin to tighten around her.

'Goodnight, drive safe.' he waved her off with a grim face and turned back to the crime scene as she drove away. What was going on? Was this a warning? Or a message?

When she reached the motel a few minutes later, she found out. Her room door was hanging open, blowing in the cold night breeze. Tentatively, and with a hammering heart, she pushed it open to see the ruin that her room had once been.

Someone had slashed the bed and sofa to pieces, the stuffing, and feathers of the innards scattered everywhere like the guts of a mutilated animal. Her clothes were strewn on the floor, trampled, filthy and cut to ribbons, her laptop shattered and discarded. Jen walked into the destruction in a daze, her mind not quite taking in the details as her eyes were fixed on the wall above her bed. Scrawled in red spray paint, a message gleamed wetly in the light that filtered in from the street.

It read, simply:

You're next

With shaking hands, Jen fumbled in her pocket for the napkin and began to dial.

*

They sat in Jack's car, looking into the Process Church compound, taking in its eerie stillness, Jen going over the plan in her head once more. Jack had told her that the spray paint warning was no idle threat, and that even if she left town now, they might still come after her. The only way to save herself was to follow his plan and find enough evidence that they could convict the Church and get it made public. Once it was out, it wouldn't be able to be hidden away and covered up again, and her celebrity for having revealed it would be its own protection. Or so he said. Jen wasn't as convinced, but she knew that the choice had already been made for her. Without meaning to, she had stumbled into something much bigger, and more terrifying than she could have known, and now to escape, she could only keep pushing forward. As the saying went, the only way out, was through. Their plan was to break into the basement together, each carrying a camera, or in Jen's case two with her button camera as well, and then separate and try to find as much, or indeed any, evidence that they could that tied the Church to the murders and disappearances. As a backup plan, Jack had a friend of his ready to contact the police if they were gone for more than 2 hours, with copies of all the evidence they currently had. They just had to hope it would be enough. If she was honest, Jen didn't think it was much of a plan, but it was better than nothing. The worst case scenario, hopefully at least, was that they found nothing. At least, that's what she told herself and tried to ignore the implications that said the worst case scenario was really going into that basement and never coming out again.

'Ready?' Jack asked, as he tested the action of the bolt cutters he'd brought with him to get through the fence. He was dressed in dark clothes, and his face held a kind of fragile determination that occasionally bordered on glee - she tried not to think too hard about his mental stability.

'As I'll ever be, let's go.' Jen said, getting out of the car, with him following suit a moment later.

They closed the car doors as quietly as they could and stole across the empty, overgrown patch of grass that led to the side of the fence that lay closest to the Church building itself. Jack made quick work of the fence, cutting a hole they could crawl through easily. They stole across the well-tended turf of the compound, moving from building to building as they made their way to the Church. No one seemed to be moving around in the compound, which given the bitter chill in the air, made sense. Still, it gave Jen a vague sense of unease, there was such a thing as too quiet. They made it to the wall of the Church without incident, and Jack began testing the windows to see which one they should break into. Above them, the lights of the Church blazed, and within Jen could hear a raised voice giving a sermon, occasionally a word or two being returned to him by the crowd. She couldn't make out the words, but something about the sound caused her to shiver; they were too guttural. A subdued crunch brought her attention back to the present, and Jack was beckoning her over. He had taped up and then broken a corner of one of the basement windows with a screwdriver, and now the window was yawning wide, leaving a letterbox shaped hole of darkness in the bottom of the building.

'You first, I'll keep watch.' he said, waving her in with his hand.

Crouching low, and swallowing the rising fear inside her, she slipped her legs into the space and lowered herself down until, with a small crunch of broken glass, she landed in the darkness of the basement.

Jen waited for a moment, surrounded by the blackness, listening for any indication of her entry being heard.

'It's fine, come on.' she whispered to the window above her, being answered a moment later by the muffled struggling of Jack as he lowered himself in as well. When he was down, they both turned on their torches, casting the beams around in the dusty air. The basement was full of old chairs and tables, a few storage shelves of paint and tools and other assorted items. Despite its unusual size, the contents of the basement weren't anything Jen would have called particularly damning or evidence of murder. Still, she was well aware that this was only part of the basement, the part that the public, and the police, would see if they ever came down here for any reason.

'There.' came Jack's quiet whisper and he pointed with his torch at a door at the back of the room. It was emblazoned with high voltage warning signs and held shut by a thick padlock and bolt that seemed excessive to keep people out of an electricity cupboard. They made their way carefully over to it, every step calculated to make the least amount of noise. Above them they could hear the congregation still going on, the low drone of the sermon's voice echoing in the open air of the basement. Jack brought out his bolt cutters again and set to work on the padlock, and after a minute, it fell away with a heavy thump to the wooden floor. He pulled the bolt free and opened the door. What hit them first was the smell. It was like a cross between a charnel house and a zoo, acrid and nausea inducing, with a kind of burning scent mixed in.

'What the hell is that?' Jen asked, looking down the darkness wreathed staircase that sat behind the door.

Jack shook his head, his eyes wide and face pale in her torch light. Placing his camera in his pocket, he reached into his waistband and pulled a gun out, checking it was loaded. Jen felt her eyes widen in shock, but didn't say anything. Despite all her reason telling her a gun was a bad idea, the scared animal in her couldn't help but take comfort in it. He began to descend the steps carefully, torch and gun held out in front of him. Jen followed close behind, her camera trained on the shrinking darkness in front of them. The stairs descended for what felt like an age until they abruptly came to a halt on a red earth floor. Shining her torch around, Jen saw they were standing in a seven foot or so high tunnel hacked straight into the sandstone under the church. There was a faint orange glow in coming from further down the tunnel, and she thought she heard something too, something that wasn't the congregation above them. It sounded like chanting or singing, and it sent horrible shivers up her spine. Treading carefully, they made their way forwards, deeper into the labyrinth, following the light and sound. They passed dark openings on either side, yawing open like toothless mouths ready to swallow them whole. Jen couldn't help but keep glancing behind her, the sensation that someone was there, just behind, but just out of sight, was constantly building.

Eventually, the tunnel opened out into a small, round room and Jen had to stop herself from screaming in fright. The room was decorated by skulls, hundreds of them, many of them broken and cracked by the violence that killed their occupant, but that wasn't why she kept her hand firmly over her mouth. Ahead of them, surrounded by candles and strange symbols forged out of metal, was an altar of some sort, and on the altar stood three heads in various stages of decomposition. One was an old woman's barely recognizable as the flesh had begun to run like molten wax, another a young boy, his jaw mostly rotted off but his eyes still glassy, accusing, and finally the head of Bob, the shopkeeper. His was fresh enough to have dripped blood onto the spike it sat on very recently, his eyes still holding the surprised expression they had when he died. Jen, feeling as though she might be sick at any moment, swept her camera over the heads, her conviction to make sure they were recognized and used against the Church burning strong.

'Wha-' came a startled cry from Jack behind her.

She turned curiously. There was a flash of a terrible masked face, a crack as something heavy hit her across the face, and stars in her eyes as she fell limply to the floor.

*

Waking came groggily, and intermittently, to her. There were flashes of being dragged through flame lit tunnels, of animal skulls leering at her, and of fire. Jen snapped awake suddenly and for a moment, her brain couldn't process where she was. She was tied, naked, by her wrists and ankles to a splintered wooden post, the thick rope already rubbing welts into her skin. The low ceiling cavern around her spread out in a circle, lit by regular flaming torches that made the air thick and hot, and she found she was already slicked with sweat. To her side, Jack was strung up naked in the same position, his head lolling unconsciously to one side, blood running down his face from an injury under his hair. In the center of the room stood a huge, black pillar that shone darkly in the torchlight, its presence feeling oppressive and cold even in the heat of the place. And around this pillar circled a group of black-robed figures, their steps timed to the incessant beating of a series of deafening drums. Each step they took, they chanted something that she couldn't understand, but the guttural sounds filled her with dread. She struggled against her bonds, hoping to loosen them, to escape, to get away from this nightmare. The drums and chanting continued, the volume and tempo increasing until she thought her head would burst, when it suddenly ceased. The cult members turned as one to a shadowed entrance where a figure emerged. It was a woman, naked herself except for an elaborate mask and headdress made up of what looked like multiple horned animals. The skulls were stained darkly with blood and only her mouth could be seen on her face. Her body told of her age, her breasts sagged low on her chest, her skin hanging, wrinkled off her bones and her pubic hair was white with her years. Still, she carried herself erect, her movements were graceful, and overwhelmingly, an almost suffocating air of power seemed to roll off of her in waves. She stalked over to Jen and looked her up and down with an approving smile.

'Welcome my dear.' her voice was cool, and cultured, and terrible, 'As you can see, we are not people to make idle threats. Yes, you will do very well indeed...'

'Please, just let me go, I'll leave town, I'll never tell anyo-' Jen was silenced by a long, thin finger on her lips.

'Shhh, the time is passed for that Jennifer, you must accept the consequences of your actions.'

The woman's gaze turned to Jack, who was just waking up, his eyes roving as he tried to work out where he was.

'Ah, and the first sacrifice awakes, good evening, Jack.'

His fear, so stark for a moment, was quickly overtaken by rage when he realized where he was, and who they were.

'You fucking bastards! You took my daughter, you took my girl away from me! I'll kill you! I'll kill you!' his yelling echoed in the chamber as he struggled against his bindings, eyes roving.

'It is right that you hate us,' said the woman, reaching out behind her and having an ancient looking, wooden handled brush put into her hand by a member of the cult. She walked over to Jack and began to draw graceful, curving symbols onto his exposed skin, 'Your hatred makes you right to open the gate.'

'What the fuck are you talking about?' he raged, his eyes burning, 'You're all crazy! How can you do this to people?'

'Quite easily,' the woman replied, reaching out her other hand, and into it was placed a long, obsidian blade, 'It is simply a matter of acting.'

With that, she sank the blade deep into Jack's belly. Jen screamed then, her throat burning as her fear made itself a physical thing she was trying to expel. Jack's eyes went wide in shock and confusion, he looked down at the knife, not seeming to realize what it was, before, with jolting, sickening movements, the woman pulled it across his belly and stepped back to let his entrails flow out like pink, bloody rope.

'Let us begin!' shouted the woman, holding the blood stained blade high.

With a kind of bestial roar and the sudden hammering of the drums, the gathered cult members cast off their robes and threw themselves forward towards Jack's bleeding and mutilated body. They began to tear at his flesh, pulling off chunks, eating them, feeding them to each other. Blood flowed thickly onto the floor and Jen found herself vomiting in both revulsion and fear. As the drums' beat continued, she found her vision starting to blur oddly at the edges, the leaping shadows of the cultists began to take on twisted new forms, the pillar in the center began to change and bulge out towards her.

'Let the bloodshed open the doorway,' the masked woman was saying, the brush back in her hand as she began to draw symbols on Jen, in what she realized was blood, 'And let this brave soul's sacrifice be our offering, come forth!'

The woman's words rang with an inhuman power, each syllable seeming to fill the chamber, and the bulge on the pillar grew and grew, extending out towards Jen. The sounds around her were deafening, the screams of the cultists mixed with her own and then, suddenly, in the chaos, there was silence as two eyes opened in the bulging pillar in front of her. They were the pitch black of the most starless night spaces, and regarded her for a moment, before a slit appeared underneath, a mouth.

The pillar smiled with a mouth full of razors, and hell opened before her.

There was a sudden, catastrophic series of bangs around her and the spell was broken. Suddenly she was back in the room, and a new kind of chaos reigned. Cultist ran in panic as armored and masked figures spilled into the room, spraying bullets from guns held high. The cultists fell, writhing and, the masked woman was gunned down as she ran to attack the invaders. Released from the hellish vision she had seen, Jen felt her consciousness fading away. In the last moments, before darkness took her, she heard a voice, friendly and reassuring, and rough, gentle hands beginning to free her bonds.

'Don't worry I've got you. You're safe now, you're safe.'

*

Jen sat up in her hospital bed, watching the latest news. The Process Church scandal was still all anyone in the media wanted to talk about. The police raid that had saved her two weeks earlier had stumbled across evidence of decades of murder, human sacrifice, brainwashing, and kidnapping. The reporter had just finished breathlessly discussing the new theory that was emerging that said that the only reason it had taken this long was due to the cult having control of the local police force. Sheriff Thomas Wilson, newly appointed from Deputy after his predecessor was discovered to be amongst those who had covered up the cult's activities, had sworn to track down every last link of the cult and eradicate it. She looked up at the card beside her bed, from the very same man, wishing her well in her recovery. Her only regret was that in the chaos and confusion of the police raid, wherever her cameras had ended up, they were yet to be found, and without them, her documentary was missing a lot of footage. Still, she had already been contacted by three separate movie studios for the rights to her story... there might be hope after all.

*

Sheriff Thomas watched the footage intently. The cultist in charge of the stolen camera had clearly enjoyed his work, taking in Jen's unconscious, naked body with the lens as they strung her up for the ritual. He flicked through the other footage, seeing the security guard, Randy and Bob, their faces frozen by the camera's lens. With a sigh he shut down the camera and pulled the memory card out, holding it between finger and thumb for a moment before throwing it onto the fire he had started in his backyard. He watched it as it melted away, surrounded by documents and evidence of every kind, his face impassive, his eyes seeing all kinds of things in the flames.

'Daddy, come inside! I want to show you my drawing!' came a small girl's voice from the open patio door behind him.

'Coming!' he replied, turning his back on the fire, a fatherly smile now arranging itself on his lips as he shut out the cold, dark night.

AVA'S NIGHTMARE

George Lim

48

Steam swirled up from the coffee cup in front of Ava. Her eyes were bloodshot from long nights at the police station. Dark circles dipped onto her cheeks. It had been a crazy couple of weeks. She laughed under her breath and shook her head.

"You ok there, Brooks?" Charlie poked his head out of his office.

"Yeah, yeah. I'm fine, Chief." Ava picked up her coffee cup and leaned back in her chair, "It's just still kind of surreal right now."

Charlie locked up his office door behind him, "We got him, kid. Go home and get some sleep, ok?"

"Yes, sir." Exhaustion spread over Ava's face as she sipped from her cup. Her coffee had made a ring around part of the morning paper's headline: *Green River Killer Captured.*

The Maple Valley Police Department had been working closely with the King County Sherriff's Office the past few years, but the murders had been going on for the past two decades. Young women murdered, their corpses violated. Some of the bodies still weren't identified yet. Most of them had been prostitutes. Ava's shoulders shuddered with a sigh of relief. The killer had been on the loose for most of her life. Even knowing he was behind bars, she still didn't feel safe. A lifetime spent looking over her shoulder, peering into dark alleyways, always making sure to park under a light. Those habits were drilled into her now. The fear of the unknown didn't vanish with a conviction. It lingered in the peripheral of her vision, waiting.

Patting her face to keep the delirium of sleep at bay, Ava grabbed her jacket and headed for the door. She paused in the doorway. The precinct was empty. Staplers were cockeyed on the corners of desks. Paperwork cluttered up baskets. The overhead lights buzzed softly. Ava leaned her forehead against the door frame and flipped off the light switch. She walked outside and locked the building behind her. The temperature was in the forties. Ava's breath clouded around her. The sudden cold helped to wake her up a bit. Her fingers fumbled in her pocket to find her car keys.

The key hole on the beat-up red Buick had a thin layer of frost over it. Ava shoved the key into the door and pried it open. It took a few moments for the frosted windshield to thaw. Her hands ached from the cold. She buried them between her legs for extra warmth until the car had enough visibility to drive. Streetlights pierced the night and burst in halos on the glass. She couldn't see any stars.

Ava's duplex was dark as she pulled into the driveway. Her neighbors were out of town for an early Christmas vacation. She scraped her boots on the door mat and flicked on the stained glass lamp to the right of the door.

"Hey, Simon," the orange tabby weaved in and out of her legs leaving cat fur on her uniform. "Sorry I was out again so late."

Ava poured some cat food in his bowl. She put her badge and gun on the counter next to a bowl of badly bruised bananas. A soft smile lingered on her lips as her eyes lit upon an old picture of her mother. It was a bittersweet moment. The wrinkles on her mom's face showed a lifetime of hard decisions. Ava had never met her dad. As far as she knew he could have been any of the Johns her mom had to turn to put food on the table. She wasn't proud of it, but she did what she had to in order to make sure she and Ava were taken care of. That's why the Green River Killer had been such an important case. In every victim's face, Ava saw her mother. Any one of those girls could have been a struggling single mom just trying to get by.

Downing a beer from the fridge, Ava stumbled towards her bedroom. "Come on, Simon. Let's hit the hay."

The two-day weekend went by way too fast. Monday morning, Ava geared up and headed back to the station. Simon sat in the living room window, tail flicking back and forth as she backed out of the driveway. The road to the station was clear of traffic. The city seemed more at ease after Ridgway was behind bars. Ava's heart skipped a beat as she pulled into her parking space. The medical examiner's car was parked out front.

The bell dinged signaling her entrance, "Hey, Reyes, why is Mike here?" She peered across the office to where the medical examiner was spreading out some pictures on the back table.

"You didn't hear yet?" Andre Reyes pushed out of his chair so he could talk lower, "Another body came up over the weekend."

"Do they think it was another GRK victim?"

Reyes shrugged, "That's the thing. Fits the pattern, but get this, M.E. places time of death two days after Ridgway was arrested."

Ava's face contorted in panic concern, "Do you think he wasn't the real killer?"

"He confessed." Reyes shook his head, "Most likely copycat killer or maybe an accomplice."

Walking briskly, Ava approached the table at the back of the room where the Chief and a few other officers were looking over crime scene pictures with Mike. She picked up one of the pictures. A young woman, no older than twenty-five was tinged blue. Her eyes were wide open. A fly had landed on her pupil when the camera had taken the image. She was naked like the rest of the victims. The picture churned Ava's stomach, "Why weren't we called when it happened?"

"Sent it to the King County Sheriffs first to have the Green River Task Force take a look at it. Seemed like something they would want to know about." Mike shook his grey head. "You know, I was hoping we were done with this now."

Charlie patted him on the back, "Go get you some coffee. I'll fill Officer Brooks in."

Ava watched Mike walk away before she spoke, "Chief, what if we got the wrong guy?"

"He confessed, Brooks. Working on a plea bargain."

"But this fits the pattern."

Charlie massaged the worry lines on his forehead, "Except for one thing. Look at her closer. What do you see?"

Studying the pictures closer, Ava wracked her brain. "She's clean."

"Yup. The last few we found were buried. Ridgway said he started burying them so he wouldn't be tempted to have sex with the bodies later. This one wasn't buried."

"Any DNA on her?"

"There was some vaginal tearing, but the culprit wore a condom, so no semen." Charlie leaned his head to the side as a voice rang out over the radio on his shoulder.

"Charlie, I think you're going to want to see this." Static crackled over the radio.

"What is it?" The Chief held down the button on the side as he replied.

"We've got three more."

Ava's heart dropped into her stomach. The drive out to the river bank made her want to throw up. Four more girls had died since Ridgway had been off the streets. Boots squelched through the mud as officers combed the fallen branches at the river's edge for any clues or evidence. Three girls were laying side by side near a pile of rocks. One of them still had pink in her cheeks. This was a fresh dump.

"Son of a—" Ava kicked a half-rotted tree stump.

"Brooks, go take five!" The Chief yelled out admonishingly and pointed to where the cruisers were parked.

Waving her arms in frustration, she stomped back to her car and paced along the side. This couldn't keep happening! So many girls had died already, and they were so close to wrapping everything up. Now there was another killer on the loose. She couldn't just sit here and watch this keep happening in her town anymore. It had eaten away at her for the last two years. Charlie had kept telling her the Task Force had the lead on this one. This was their territory. But now? The Green River Killer was behind bars now. This was a new killer. Up for grabs.

"Brooks, you doing ok?" Reyes sat on the hood of her police car.

"I can't keep doing this, Andre."

"Well, what do you have in mind?" He ran his hand through his dark brown hair and looked at her while she moved frantically back and forth.

Ava pursed her lips, "I'm sick of us playing tag along. What if we've been going about this the wrong way? Going from body to body waiting on the next victim...We need to get in front of this. We need to get someone on the inside."

"How?" There was a slight scoff to his voice.

"What if someone went undercover?"

"Who would be dumb enough—" Andre paused, "No. No way. You can't put yourself at risk like that."

"We put ourselves at risk every day!"

"Not like that. That would be walking into a lion's den."

"I can't sit on the sidelines anymore." Ava bit her bottom lip and looked back towards the river bank, "Someone has to help them."

Charlie was taking long strides in their direction, "You calmed down any?"

"Put me under cover." Ava's voice was brash and brazen. Her eyes shone out fiercely. Rocks rolled under her feet as she took a more authoritative stance. Feet apart, shoulders back.

Wrinkles and bristly eyebrows matted across the Chief's brow, "Ava, I know these cases are important to you." His voice was gentle and compassionate, "But right now you're too emotionally involved. I can't put you out in the field like this." He shook his head apologetically, "I can't have that on my conscience."

Charlie turned and walked back towards the river bank. Hot tears brimmed in Ava's eyes. She could do this! She *needed* to do this. She felt sick in her stomach that she had put herself out on a limb and been turned down. It was like the Chief was telling her she wasn't good enough. Her teeth ground into one another as she watched him walk away. She was strategically avoiding Andre's gaze. If she made eye contact the dam inside her would burst, and her tears would overwhelm her.

They stood there in silence for a moment. The sound of rushing water mingled with the braying barks of the K-9 unit. A frigid breeze cut across their cheeks. Andre shifted his weight on the hood of the car, "You know he cares about you, right?"

"Sometimes I wish he didn't." Ava climbed in her police car and threw it in reverse. Andre leapt off of the hood and staggered a few steps away as she spun out of the gravel clearing driving back towards town.

Charlie had been like a dad to her even before her mom had passed away. She had lost count of how many times he had tried to get her mom to get her life together. She never brought the men home with her, so at least there was that, but between the bruises and the track marks Adeline Brooks had been fighting a losing battle. Charlie was the one who had come to the house the morning her mother died to break the news. Heroin overdose. Since then, the officers had been Ava's second family. They made sure she was taken care of, and not long after her mom's passing, Ava applied to the police academy. Fresh out of high school and determined not to make her mother's mistakes, she sailed through the obstacle courses and classes. Years later she still felt like she had to prove she was worthy to be on the force. The chip on her shoulder from Adeline's death still weighed heavily on her. If she had been a stronger daughter, maybe she could have helped her mom stay clean. If she had gotten an after-school job, maybe her mom wouldn't have had to sell herself to pay the rent. Ava blamed herself for the depression that overtook Adeline and pushed her towards the dependency. A single mom with no support system. The pressure and isolation had eventually led to the overdose.

Stopped at a red light in town, Ava saw a young woman dressed in skimpy attire duck around the corner of a building. She was getting off the street at the sight of the cruiser. Trying to avoid a confrontation.

She had to be freezing in this weather. Smoke trailed up from a cigarette butt the girl had dropped on the sidewalk. When the light turned green, Ava passed the gap between buildings the girl had disappeared into. There were a few other girls in there with her. All of them were in short skirts and low-cut tops, shivering in the alley. Ava's fingers tightened on the steering wheel. She hadn't been able to save her mother, but she could still save these girls.

Simon purred happily around her feet as she walked into the living room. Ava punched in Charlie's number as she walked to her bedroom and flung open her closet. She flipped through the hangers holding her uniforms until she was at the far end. "Hey, Charlie, it's Brooks. I was thinking about what you said earlier, and I think it might be good for me to take a few weeks off and clear my head." Her fingers closed on a hanger holding a leopard print miniskirt. "Mmmhmm, ok. Thanks, Chief." The line went dead. Ava pulled out the miniskirt and a button-up blouse.

The next day, Ava put on extra make-up and pulled the skirt into place. She was going undercover even if she had to do it on her own. She had dropped her cruiser off at the station yesterday. Today she opened the garage and backed her mom's old, blue Toyota out. It was ancient, but less recognizable than her own red car. Dust coated the dash board, and the engine churned a few times before it started up. Adeline's favorite radio station boomed to life. Ava turned the radio down and headed for a parking lot behind the old pool joint. Goosebumps scaled her skin as she stepped out into the cold and sauntered over to the alley near the side door that led into the pool hall. A girl with ratted blonde hair and sunken eyes was leaning against the brick wall.

"Hey!" The girl pushed off from the wall and made a beeline for Ava, "This is my spot. You go get your own!" The girl pulled a knife out of her bag and flicked it open.

Ava staggered backwards, "Whoa, hey. I'm just...I'm just trying to score some H, ok?" Ava made her voice raspy and slowed her normal speaking rate. "I just need some H or some cash so I can pay a guy." She nodded her head down like she had seen her mother do countless times.

The girl paused and looked Ava up and down before putting her knife away, "You trying to get heroine?"

"Yeah, yeah, that's what I said, you know?" Ava's heart was racing already.

"Alright, ok. I'll make you a deal." The girl licked her lips. "You can stay, and any money we make will go to me. Any guy that's got H, you can have it. And," the girl scratched her arm, "if we don't get any heroine, I'll give you enough for your next hit, alright?"

It was a shit deal, but a junkie would do anything for the next fix, "Alright." Ava nodded her head and smiled goofily. "I'm Ava, by the way."

"Steph." The blonde walked back over to the wall and leaned against it again.

"How many guys you get a day here?" Ava fidgeted with her hair.

"Depends. Some days one or two. Some five or six. Business usually picks up around the holidays. Guys start feeling lonely and need a little extra comfort."

Cars drove by on the street. Steph took a few drags off of a cigarette and crossed her arms. Ava watched her from the corner of her eye, "You got family?"

"Nah. Mom's in jail for killing my dad. Only child. You?"

"Just my cat."

"Ya know, maybe it's better that way. Animals are the best kind of people." Steph smiled with the cigarette between her lips. "What's its name?"

"Simon."

"Had a turtle once. Dad found it on the side of the road. That was the only pet I ever had growing up. Named him Soup."

"You named your turtle Soup?" Ava laughed.

Steph shrugged her shoulders, "Dark sense of humor."

A black car pulled up behind the pool hall and rolled down its window. Steph walked over to the window and leaned down. Ava saw her take a wad of cash and stuff it in her bag before opening the door. She looked over her shoulder and mouthed, 'back in ten.' Ava's stomach churned. She didn't want to let Steph go with this guy knowing there was a killer on the loose, but if she said anything she would blow her cover. Ava held her breath as the car pulled out of the parking lot. She memorized the license plate as he drove out of sight.

It was unnerving that girls would just climb into a stranger's car and perform sexual acts with them. This is what her mom had done. It made her sick to think about it. Maybe Charlie was right. Maybe she was too emotionally involved in this. Shaking her head, Ava took a deep breath to steady her nerves. She needed to fight down that urge to flee and hold on to her anger.

Ten minutes seemed like an hour by the time Steph got back to the alley way. She pulled some lip balm out of her bag and rubbed it on her lips. She held out her hand and offered it to Ava, "Want some?"

"Uh, no thanks," Ava shook her head disinterestedly. Guiltily, she pushed back the thought that she might get herpes if she shared ChapStick with this girl.

"Anybody come by while I was gone?"

"Nope."

Steph tugged her skirt back down a little more, "Good."

The sun was starting to go down. After-work traffic flooded the busy street on one side of the alley. Inside the pool hall they could hear balls bouncing off of tables, and rock music hummed through the walls. Ava's arms and legs were numb. She and Steph had naturally huddled closer to one another to try and conserve body heat. Headlights reflected off of the side of a dumpster beside them. The driver flashed the lights. Steph's teeth chattered as she walked over to the car. Ava could tell she and the driver were discussing something. Steph didn't seem too happy about whatever it was.

After a minute, Steph stood up and walked back over to Ava. "This guy wants to do doubles." She looked as though she had taken a drink of spoiled milk, "Look, I haven't ever done a double before, but he's willing to pay extra for us both."

Ava's intuition was curdling at the sight of this car. She couldn't see inside, but something felt off. She nodded her head and bit her lip. Steph couldn't go off alone with this guy, "Ok, yeah."

"Yeah?" Steph looked surprised and a little relieved.

"Yeah," Ava repeated herself with more conviction.

The two girls walked to the car together. Ava fought her instinct to run. Steph climbed in the front seat as Ava slid in the back. The guy in the driver's seat was wearing wire rimmed glasses. He had thick blonde hair combed over to one side. His face was more handsome than Ava had been expecting. She always thought of Johns as slightly overweight, balding, middle aged men. This guy was probably in his thirties. The interior of the car smelled of leather with a faint hint of fast food. His eyes locked on Ava through the rearview mirror. He adjusted his glasses. Trying to hide her discomfort, Ava massaged warmth back into her arms. The car's heater was the only part about this that was even remotely comforting. Charlie would kill her if he knew she was doing this.

"Where are we going?" Steph tugged her seatbelt into a more comfortable position.

"Not far," the driver's voice was a soft tenner. The mildness of his tone caught Ava off guard.

They drove until they reached an abandoned lumber mill. He put the car in park, and Steph unbuckled her seatbelt. She reached over to his lap and started to undo his pants, but he grabbed her wrist. Ava's heart beat quicker as she watched from the backseat. She didn't want to see this, much less participate. What had she gotten herself into?

"Not here," he placed Steph's hand back in her own lap and climbed out of the car.

"Well, where do you want to do this? It's freezing out there!" The sun had almost disappeared as Steph tried to keep the rendezvous contained in the car.

"I want to go inside." He jerked his head towards the door of the lumber mill, "I'm paying you well enough. Get your assess inside."

"You've got to be kidding me." Steph rolled her eyes and shoved her door open with an exasperated sigh.

Ava opened her door warily. The dirt parking lot was packed solid. The temperature was dropping even more. The guy motioned for her and Steph to go through the rusted metal door. The hairs on the back of Ava's neck were standing up. This was bad. There was little light in the building. Streams of fading sunlight crept through cracks in the walls. It smelled like sawdust and mold. Steph shuddered beside her. As Ava's eyes adjusted to the dim interior, she heard a small click behind her. The sound froze her in place.

"Get on your knees." The guy pressed the barrel of a gun to Ava's back.

"Oh shit!" Steph whispered weakly, half turning her head to see what was happening. Her voice broke, "Please, please don't. We'll do whatever you want for free, ok?"

"Shut up and get on your knees!" He turned the gun on Steph who choked back a sob.

Ava slowly sank to her knees. Cold cement bit into her kneecaps and shins. The man circled around them. Ava's eyes darted around the room trying to find anything she might be able to use as a weapon. A few shoddy pieces of two by four were scattered a few feet away. A wooden pallet was propped against the side of the building. Nothing in arm's reach. She closed her eyes and tried to calm herself down enough to think. The sound of a zipper unzipping made her open her eyes. The man was fondling himself inside of his pants. Ava cringed and looked away. She had to think of something to get them out of here.

"Come here," he motioned for Steph to move closer.

Sobbing softly, Steph scooted closer to him. Ava heard the man sigh followed by slight sucking noises. She forced herself to glance up. The man had one hand on the back of Steph's head, and the other with the gun was resting on the top of his own head. His eyes were closed. Steph gagged and tried to pull away from him, but he kept her where she was. Ava was able to catch Steph's eye. Tears were streaming down her face. She looked terrified. With one more glance to make sure his eyes were still closed, Ava made a silent chomping gesture with her teeth. Steph's fear was causing her to shake. Ava could see her struggling to muster the will power before she opened her mouth wider and clamped her jaw down. A shot rang out as the man squeezed the trigger automatically, his body recoiling in pain. He screamed in utter agony, and blood spurted from where Steph's teeth had ripped through him.

Before he could recover, Ava charged at his knees and knocked him onto his back. The gun skittered across the floor. He was having trouble breathing, and his arms fought more to curl towards his wound than they did to get Ava off of him. She managed to flip him over and pull his arms behind his back. Her foot pressed into the center of his back. The pain became too much, and his body went limp. Blood slowly spread across the floor near his waist. Steph was spitting profusely trying to get the taste out of her mouth. She was shaking from adrenaline and from the cold.

"Find his phone!" Ava yelled at Steph to bring her back to the moment.

"I-I don't know where it is!" The girl fumbled through his pockets, "We need to leave. We gotta get out of here!" Her numb fingers finally wrestled the phone out of his left pocket.

"Call the police," Ava's own breathing was shuddering now.

"Are you crazy?! They'll send us to jail! We're a prostitute and a junkie. They'll never believe us!"

"I'm a cop! Call them."

"What? Holy shit. Holy shit!" Steph punched in the number and ran her fingers through her hair, pacing nervously. "Yes, hello? There was—I'm—" She pulled the phone away from her face and looked at Ava in panic, "I don't know what to say!"

Ava jerked the phone from her hand, "This is Officer Ava Brooks. I need Maple Valley P.D. at the old lumber mill. Suspect was injured during apprehension. Send an ambulance!" She tossed the phone to the ground. "Steph, I need you to remain calm, ok? Can you do that for me?"

"You're a freaking cop! Listen, Ava, please don't send me to jail, please! I didn't mean to hurt him that bad, I was just so scared."

"Calm down! He had a gun on us. It was self-defense." Ava needed to get her calm. She was starting to hyperventilate, "Just breathe, ok?"

"Ok," Steph took deep, ragged breaths trying to regain her composure.

Within minutes, police sirens echoed in the distance followed by an ambulance. Charlie came through the door with his gun drawn, "Put your hands up!" He barked his order at Steph and glanced to Ava. Over Steph's renewed panic, he called out to Ava, "What happened? You were supposed to be on vacation!"

"I lied!" Ava yelled back as two EMT's came in to assess the man's wounds. Grabbing Charlie's handcuffs, she secured the man's wrists behind his back before she let go of him. "I had to do this, Chief. I couldn't sit back and let more women die because of sick people like this guy!" Out of the corner of her eye, she saw Reyes bag the suspect's gun for evidence.

"Well what the hell happened here?" Charlie's face was red with anger.

"I put myself undercover and ran into Steph," Ava gestured to the blonde girl the EMT's were leading outside with a blanket wrapped around her. "This John wanted us both to go with him, and when we got here he pulled a gun on us. Forced Steph into oral sex, and she bit him out of self-defense."

Charlie winced, "Jezuz, Brooks." He shook his head.

"Hey, Chief? You might want to come over here." Reyes called out.

Ava and Charlie walked to where Andre's voice had come from. He was standing behind a pile of rotted two-by-fours. A girl was laying behind the wood pile. She couldn't be more than seventeen. Reyes leaned down and pressed his fingers into her neck. There was a faint pulse beneath his fingertips.

"I need an EMT over here now!" Andre's voice boomed across the room.

A woman in scrubs ran over to them and started taking vitals. "She's still alive, but barely." Surprise echoed in her voice as she sprang into action.

"It has to be him!" Ava shot darts with her eyes towards the unconscious man being bandaged.

"We don't know that yet." Charlie shook his head at her again.

Ava stared at him incredulously, "Seriously! Look where we are! Look at this girl!"

"It's all circumstantial right now. We must have something to tie him to this and the other murders. We can't convict him just because he brought you to where an almost dead girl was."

"Check his car! Check through here! There has to be something." Ava's frustration was seizing her chest.

"Reyes, get her out of here. Take her home." Charlie waved her away dismissively. His actions were like a dagger in her heart.

Reyes pulled off his jacket and slung it over Ava's shoulders. It was still warm as she pulled her arms into it, "What do you think?" She climbed sullenly into the passenger seat of Andre's car.

"Well," he fired up the heater and pulled away from the old lumber mill, "I think even if he isn't the guy we've been looking for, you still helped to get a bad person off of the street. I think those two girls are only alive right now because of you. Try not to let Chief get to you, ok?"

Ava stewed in her anger and aggravation, "I just want so badly to make a difference here."

"To those girls you made a hell of a difference."

"I just don't want anyone else to die."

A half smile curved Andre's lips, "That's why most of us become policemen. To stop the bad guys. Save people. You're too hard on yourself." He glanced over at her.

"What do you think is going to happen now?"

"We'll just have to see what the evidence says. Who knows? Maybe you did help catch the second killer."

Andre dropped Ava off at home. Simon greeted her as usual. As the headlights backed out of her drive, Ava scooped up Simon and let herself cry into his fur. Her arms were still shaking. Her mom had put herself in those kinds of situations all the time to take care of her. She cried from exhaustion and emotional stress. She cried because even if this guy was the killer, she would still feel inadequate inside. Ava thought if she could save lives she would finally feel worthy of her badge, but right now all she felt was small and alone. Simon purred contentedly in her lap. Eventually, she cried herself to sleep still wearing Andre's jacket.

The next few days were stressful. She had been cut off from knowing what was going on in the investigation. Her statement had been videotaped and reviewed. She wasn't allowed to know the evidence surrounding the case since technically she had been working against orders. Andre was coming over after his shift today to pick up his jacket. Ava scrambled to gather up the half-empty beer bottles around her duplex before he came over.

A car pulled into the driveway followed by Andre's knock. Ava called through the door, "Come in!"

He stepped inside and wiped his feet on the mat. Simon flicked his tail sleepily on the back of the couch, "Hey."

"Any news?"

Andre scowled slightly, "Can't really tell you much, but the girl we found woke up today."

"How's she doing?"

"Alright, considering." He shrugged and sat down on the couch. Simon's tail curled casually around Andre's face. Reyes tried to shoo the tail away, but Simon was persistent.

"Any idea when they are going to charge him, or if they are going to charge him?"

Andre nodded, "D.A. is talking with him. They think we should know more in a few days."

"Ok." Ava frowned and picked up his jacket, "Sorry, it's got some cat hair on it."

"Eh, that's alright." Andre pushed himself up and took the jacket from her.

"Thanks for loaning it to me the other night, by the way."

"No problem." Andre waved goodbye and headed out the door. Ava followed and closed it behind him.

The next day she received a call from Charlie asking her to come down to the police station. Her stomach tossed and turned the whole way there. She hadn't really been able to eat too much since the night everything happened. Ava took a deep breath and trudged into the station. A few people stared at her as she walked in. Other avoided looking at her all together. She bit her lip and rapped her knuckles on the Chief's door.

"Yep, come in." He was shuffling through paperwork as she walked into his office. He glanced up at her, "Close the door behind you."

"What's going on, Chief?" Ava closed the door with a click behind her and sat across from Charlie.

"Well, Brooks, I wanted to be the first to tell you that the man you apprehended—Elan Parker—confessed to the murders of those four girls we found."

A sigh of relief exploded from Ava, "I *knew* it had to be him!"

"Hang on, I'm not done yet."

"Yes, sir. Sorry, sir." She tucked her hand into her lap and looked at the tops of her knees.

"Turns out that Parker attended the same church as Ridgway. Shared some of his same ideals. Once Ridgway was arrested, Parker took it on himself to," Charlie motioned with air quotes, "carry on the vision and rid the world of the unclean women." He mumbled under his breath, "Self-righteous prick."

"So what happens now?"

"Well, he's going to jail. D.A. is just battering around details of his sentence now. Trying to see if he can help find any other victims that Ridgway may not have revealed yet."

"Ok," Ava nodded determinedly. She felt as though she had made some progress towards proving herself.

"Parker isn't the only reason I wanted to talk to you today."

Ava's heart sank from the pain that crossed momentarily across the Chief's face. "What is it?" Apprehension filled her gut.

"You went directly against my orders in doing this, Ava. You put yourself and members of the public in danger because of your actions."

"I saved two girls' lives!" Ava pushed away from the desk and stood up.

"I know," he held his hands up defensively, "but that doesn't change the fact that you went against orders. I have to suspend you."

"Unbelievable! I helped you find a killer before he killed anyone else." She leaned down towards him. Her blood was boiling.

"Brooks, I'm going to have to ask you to watch your tone." Charlie stood up, towering above her.

Ava clenched her jaw and shook her head, "I can't believe this. How long is my suspension?"

"Two months."

"Two months! Are you kidding me?"

"During that time, I set up a place for you to volunteer at the Vine Maple Place. I think it might help you get in touch with your core beliefs a little better. You also have to see a psychologist to deal with any residual trauma from that night in the lumber mill, and honestly maybe some issues you're having still from the loss of your mother."

Vine Maple Place was an organization that helped families find their feet after hardships. It also helped kids that were on the path to living on the street. Kids that might one day end up like Steph if not for some extra help. Ava nodded and left his office in silence.

Maybe Charlie was right. Maybe this was what she needed right now. Volunteering there would give her a sense of accomplishment and the knowledge that she was making a difference in the lives of those families. It was more of an immediate spiritual reward than trailing a criminal from body to body and just hoping to stop them before someone else was killed. She knew she was meant to make a difference in the world. She had come too far to fall under the shadow of the heartache that men like Ridgway and Parker cast. She was determined to fight against the current.

TO YOUR GRAVE

JENNY COVINGTON

Anna's life never looked like it could fall apart like other people's lives did.

She and Jake, her boyfriend of ten years, lived the perfect DINK lifestyle. Dual income, no kids. Free to use their money as they pleased and live an easy life. They looked like the typical hipster couple. Anna was blonde, long and lithe. She had the build of a gazelle and was one of the best cross country runners during her high school years. Jake had tattoos on both arms and managed a department at Peet's coffee. Making a combined income of over six-figures, they could save. They were considering using their savings to roam the world, then working another ten years and buying a house. Which would sort of make up for Anna's dreary job at the dairy plant. It wasn't anything glamorous, no dairy plant work could realistically be considered glamorous. And it wasn't interesting or exciting either, just the office work that kept the plant in order. Accounts, moving books, telling people when they were too early or late... The only true highlight was her friend, Tina.

And today Tina was late, as usual.

"It's like you don't take your work seriously." Anna sighed. "You're late by a whole hour today. I should be giving you a form to fill in."

"But you won't, cause I'm cute." Tina pulled an exaggerated pout before collapsing into her chair and putting on the kettle. A petite young woman at five-two, she looked up to Anna in more ways than one. Her big brown eyes and ivory skin got her plenty of suitors in the office, even some of the married men couldn't help but ask her out. "Coffee?"

Anna nodded. "Sure, let's have a refill."

"Can't stay mad at me?" Tina laughed as she reached for her favorite flavor, pumpkin, in the cupboard. She scooped out the brownish-orange powder and poured it into two cups of hot water.

"Not when you're making coffee... Besides, it's not like anyone saw you."

"*Thank you.*" Tina muttered in a sing-song voice, stirring the brew.

"I wish I could sound as alert and happy as you."

"Just sleep an extra four or five hours, it'll be fine," Tina laughed.

"If only I had the time..."

Tina shrugged and handed Anna the hot cup. "It's not like you don't make enough money, why not have a break?"

Anna shook her head. "Nah, Jake and I almost have enough for our round the world year. It's taken a bit, but we'll make it."

Tina shook her head. "Ten years of savings to blow in a year." She blew at the steam over her coffee then took a sip. "Mmmmm. I am the best and my coffee is the best."

Anna laughed, it wasn't like little home grown Tina would get it. "Well, we had the plan, save for ten years, travel the world. Save another ten years, get a house. Save another ten years, retire."

Tina nodded. "I guess it gets easier as your salaries go up. But it'll be wrecked when you have kids. My sister has three and they're eating her out of house and home."

Anna scowled. "No kids, no way." Not for her, at least. She wanted to live a freer, happier life than that.

"You say that *now*," Tina said, testing the heat of the coffee again, "but most folks I know are changing their minds already. The baby bug can still get you."

Anna shook her head and smiled. "Not me. I'll get a dog." She laughed a bit and they both settled in for work. No, she wouldn't ever want kids. She was twenty six now, she'd be thirty six when they had a house and forty six when they retired. No time in there to change nappies and run around after babies. Although... "I suppose we might need to spend some money on marriage." Anna added almost wistfully.

"Marriage?" Tina looked up over her computer. "Has Jake proposed?"

Anna shook her head. "No, but he's bound to, isn't he? I mean, we've been together ten years now, since we went to that Summer camp.

We've pretty much followed each other around everywhere. We've lived together for four years. Why not get married?"

Tina shook her head and laughed a bit.

"What's that about?" Anna growled. She never liked it when Tina, home grown, immature, less educated Tina, acted so condescending.

"He just doesn't seem like the type to root down." She replied. "Remember when I first met him?"

Anna nodded. "You said he looked like the polygamous type and said we wouldn't last."

"Well, I still get that vibe from him. He doesn't feel like the sort of guy who'd marry."

"Well, you were wrong about that and you're wrong now. I bet he wants to propose somewhere nice on holiday." Anna retorted.

Tina raised her eyebrows sarcastically and sipped her coffee.

She didn't give it much more thought over the day, but on her way home, Anna felt doubt and anger building up inside her. Sure, Jake never seemed like the monogamous type. Not to her, not to Tina and not to anyone. At camp everyone knew he was the guy who got into tens of teen panties and for some reason most of the girls were proud of it. And he was a disgusting flirt at all times. But their relationship had been on better grounds. Anna had held back for months to make sure he could be loyal to her and Jake seemed willing to work hard for a real relationship with her. She had followed his university choice and later crossed the country to find work in the town where he was hired. Of course he would be loyal to her. He had to be...

But little things were starting to nag at her. The flirting. The late nights. The lack of an engagement, or even a promise ring. She had bought them both promise rings and wore hers religiously. But his rested on his bedside table at all times.

She would start light. As soon as she got home she made a beeline for the bedroom and then for the living room, where Jake sat in his boxers, watching TV.

"Hi sweetie." He said. "Busy day?"

"Mad busy." Anna grinned. "By the way, seeing as we're going abroad in a few months, I'd really, really like you to start wearing this." She handed him the ring.

He looked it over and put it down on the table. "You know I don't do jewellery, sweetie."

"But this is different." Anna insisted. "It's like that necklace you wore for your mother. You **wore** that so she knew you cared about her cause, right?"

"Yeah, but why wear a stupid ring to show I'm your boyfriend?"

"To keep the other girls away, to show you care about me."

Jake laughed. "I *do* care about you Anna... But people wear these if they plan on marrying and, to be honest, I never said I wanted to marry you."

Anna was taken aback, for a few seconds she didn't know what to say and fiddled with her ring. "But, you want to be with me forever, right?"

"Of course, just not married." Jake put the ring down on the table.

"And only me, right?"

Jake fell silent. "I've said I'm not comfortable having this talk." He finally said. This was what he always said when she brought up marriage, commitment or past girlfriends.

"But I just need to know. All you have to say is 'only you sweetie' and I'm good." She shrugged.

Jake shrugged back and continued watching the TV. He was unbelievable. Anna turned and walked into the kitchen to make dinner. How could he be like that? How could he be so stubborn, so non committal. He said he wanted to be with her forever. They had plans for a life together into his fifties. Sure, he didn't have to marry or wear the ring, but she'd like him to at least acknowledge her as his girlfriend, as his life partner. Especially before they went on holiday together. She sighed as she chopped the onions. Did he have to be so difficult?

She heard a knock on the edge of the kitchen door frame. She ignored him.

He walked up behind her and hugged her. "Come on sweetie, don't be like that."

She sighed. "What is it with you and commitment?"

She felt him shrug as he held her. "Do you want me to be honest?"

"Of course, always."

"I've never been a one-chick man. I've never had to commit to one person. And I don't like the idea of promising anyone forever."

"But we're making all these plans together... I get the marriage thing, with divorce stats and all, but..." Anna sighed. It was awkward to put her thoughts into words.

She felt Jake sigh as well. "Anna, I can't promise you commitment. It's not what I do. You've been my only girl most of the time, and always been my main girl, but I can't say there isn't anyone else, that there will never be anyone else or that they're just one night things, I..."

Anna turned in his arms and pushed him back. "You *what*?"

"Sweetie, I figured you knew. I mean, everyone knows, right? My brain likes you and my heart knows you're the one, but my dick, he..."

"Who is she?" Anna asked. She couldn't believe it. He was seeing another girl? "How long?"

"Well, them... pretty much from the start. I mean, you didn't expect me to go for months without, did you? I figured that was what you wanted... you got the relationship, I got the sex."

Anna moved forward and shoved him hard. He fell over on his back. "You're a worthless, lying cunt. I can't believe I trusted you for so long. I can't believe I didn't notice..." She stopped. She couldn't believe she hadn't noticed the look on his face. The blood. She looked down at her hand. The knife was in it, dripping red. The blood pooled under him and around the tear in his belly. His eyes stared blankly at the ceiling. His chest was still.

Anna let out a choked, squeaky gasp and dropped the knife, backing herself up against the counter, trying to get away from that horrible scene. She had killed him. She had killed Jake. She hadn't meant to. But she had.

She looked at the flecks of blood on her hands and, edging her way around the body, ran to the bathroom to wash them. She scrubbed until her skin was grazed and her hands were pink and swollen. She then collapsed next to the sink. What next? What next? Her mind raced. She'd just killed someone. She'd go to jail. No holidays around the world, no home together, nothing. Not to mention that without Jake it would all seem hollow and meaningless...

But for now she had to hide the evidence. Reluctantly looking at her freshly cleaned hands, she gazed out the door. She had to do something. But what? She contemplated a story she read online a few weeks back about a man who killed his wife and, rather than dispose of the body, ate the flesh. But her stomach turned. She couldn't eat Jake. And throwing him in the bin would be obvious. They would probably be able to track him back to her eventually. For now... for now he had to stay in the flat.

Carefully avoiding looking into the kitchen, Anna made her way to the bedroom and dug out a large suitcase. It was the one they had planned on using for their round-the-world trip. They were going to share it. She smiled a little. Oh well, it was all for him now. She threw out the few items in the bottom of it and made her way to the kitchen, half expecting him to be stood there, finishing making dinner. But the onions were still half chopped and Jake still lay there, paler than before, with the knife by his foot. Anna swallowed hard. This would take some doing.

She opened the suitcase on the floor beside Jake and tried to lift him. His cold body was much heavier than she ever remembered him being. Blood smeared down her arms and front. He was too heavy. Too heavy. She dropped him again and he splattered his own blood across the tiles. She resisted the urge to run back to the bathroom for a shower. She looked at the case. The blood would spread through it and ruin it.

She searched through the kitchen drawers for bin bags and carefully lined the case with them, bag after bag, layer after layer, again and again. Satisfied, she looked at Jake. She would start with the legs. They lifted into the bag surprisingly easily, although as she moved his limbs she noticed a wet, brownish pool in the blood and the stench of feces. She had to persevere. Using his knees as a lever, she managed to lift his hip up and into the bag. His lower portions occupied most of it. She carefully rearranged and bent his legs until there was more room. Then she moved to his shoulders and forced his back into the case. She curled him over himself and wedged his arms in as best she could.

Layering more towels and plastic bags over his body, she covered his face last of all before zipping up the case. It would have to stay there for now. It was heavy. She was tired. She glanced at the massive stain on the floor. And she had work to do.

She knew that piles of bloody paper towels in their tiny apartment bin would raise suspicion. So she gathered all but one of the remaining dark towels and a few dark bedsheets and used them to soak the blood up. After half an hour, she passed the last clean bed sheet over the floor. It was sparkling. They were all thrown in the bathtub and she put the shower on full, undressing before throwing her clothes into the pile and stepping in with a bottle of detergent.

Under the scalding hot shower, she scrubbed at each item until the water ran clear off it. Then, she put them into a pile to take to the washing machine. By the end her hands were sore and red again and she could hardly stand, she was so sick, aching and shaky. She wobbled to her feet under the shower head and meticulously scrubbed every inch of her skin clean before stepping out and wrapping herself in the last dark brown towel.

Once the laundry was on she felt much better. She looked from the bathroom to the kitchen and found no specks of blood from the dirty sheets and towels. She checked the kitchen and the sight of the suitcase reassured her. She picked up the knife from the floor and rinsed it under the hot tap before mopping the floor with scalding water from the kettle and making herself a cup of tea with what was left. She nodded to herself as she looked over the kitchen floor, hearing the washing machine hum in the background.

Looking at the clock, she saw it was half past ten already. Where did the time go?

She took her tea with her into the bedroom, roughly dried her hair with the towel, and got into bed. Turning off the light, she curled up tightly on her side of the bed, as far from Jake's side as she could get, and cried herself to sleep.

The next morning she could hardly move. It all felt like a bad dream and she was hoping to roll over and see Jake asleep next to her. But she was scared of not finding him there. Or of finding him there, dead and unmoving. So she lay on her side of the bed, the alarm on her phone screaming at her, louder each time. She could have sworn she felt movement on the other side of the bed and it made her curl up tighter.

As the light between the curtains grew brighter, so did her courage. She rolled over, bracing herself for whatever she might find there... Nothing. The bed was empty besides her. His side was undisturbed. She breathed a sigh of half relief and glanced from her tea, to his empty bedside table, to the time on her still screaming phone. She had fifteen minutes to make it to work on time. Fifteen minutes to check the laundry, the bathroom and the kitchen again, get dressed, grab her things and go to work.

"Come on Anna, we have to get back to normal." She told herself. She stood up and turned her alarm off. She swallowed the bitter, cold tea from her bedside table, down to the lime scaled dregs. *"I'll get dressed and ready first."* She told herself, reaching for her clothes. But of course they were in the laundry. She went to the wardrobe and tried to ignore Jake's coats as she grabbed herself a new dress and blouse. She got

dressed first, then went to the bathroom to brush her teeth, do her hair and put on her make-up. It looked bare. Too bare. Of course it did. All the towels were in the washing machine or the laundry pile. She would have to do more laundry when she got back.

The living room was harder than she'd thought. He had apparently put a game on last night and it was there, still on pause, some character stood there waving a sword in the same motion over and over. The controller rested on the table. The remote on Jake's favourite sofa pillow, which was next to the neat pile of yesterday's work clothes and the not so neat pile of unopened mail. Anna moved to turn the TV off. It was hard. But it felt better once it was done. She walked past the kitchen, not looking in, as she collected her shoes from the hallway and slipped into them.

For a moment she struggled with the choices of going into work without looking at the kitchen, or checking, just to make sure it wasn't all a dream. But it wasn't a dream, and as the image of Jake's corpse folded up in that suitcase brought tears to her eyes, she realized that if she was going to make it through the day she would have to wait to see him again.

She grabbed her handbag and her keys. But she would see him again. Just once more. She would unzip him and look at him once more before she worked out where to bury him.

On the drive into work she felt strangely collected, calm, together. Was it really this easy? She hadn't wanted to, hadn't intended to, but was it really this easy to kill someone? Was she really going to get away with it? In the books they talked about the guilt and that feeling that someone somewhere knew. But nobody knew. There had been no screams, no row. The neighbours would have barely heard them talking. She had raised her voice a bit near the end, but nothing else. And he died so soon when the knife pierced him. She hadn't even screamed after that, she hadn't had the energy.

The people at work would be expecting him. They may call her when he didn't answer his phone. But she could say something... anything. What could she say? He had gone to work? No, that would be too obvious. Someone could easily disprove that, especially as his car was in the drive. She could say they had an argument and he went for a walk. That she had noticed the car was still there and assumed he was staying with a girlfriend. After all, everyone knew he had girlfriends, right?

When she got to work and went to put the kettle on, she saw her hands were, in fact, shaking. When had this started? They weren't like that in the car...

"Good morning Anna."

Anna jumped and turned to see Tina. She must have stared, because Tina looked startled herself.

"What's the matter?" Tina asked.

"You're early." Anna improvised.

Tina burst out laughing. "Can't I be here on time for once?"

Anna shook her head. "No, it's good. Coffee?"

Tina nodded and unpacked her bag. "Why are your hands so shaky?"

"The shock of having someone other than me in here."

"What did you think it was? A ghost?" Tina laughed some more.

Anna froze again. No, of course not... She sighed and tried to steady her hands as she made the coffees.

"Something's different." Tina said as Anna handed her the coffee.

"No, it's the usual blend."

"I mean with you." Tina looked Anna square in the eye.

Anna shrugged, looked to her feet, then back up. She had to come up with something... anything... or at least use the planned argument. What was it? She sighed. "I think Jake left me."

"Oh my God, no." Tina put her coffee down. "How? Why?"

"Well, I asked him to wear the ring, we argued, he said he wanted more freedom in a relationship and he left. Normally he goes for a walk, but he wasn't back this morning. He's probably with that girl." Anna sighed again.

"You'll be fine without him. You two were pretty independent anyway, right?"

Anna nodded. "Yeah, to be honest I'm glad." Was she really glad? That he was gone? Yes. That he was dead? Maybe. No, she couldn't be. She shook her head and sighed again. "I'll manage."

"Attagirl."

The rest of the work day wasn't so bad. Nobody called her from Jake's work in the end. And she didn't have anyone guessing Jake was dead. She just didn't talk about him and felt her hands go shaky now and again. But other than that it was fine. Even the drive home went as usual.

It was on the way up the stairs that she felt nervous again. Like she would open the door and see him staring at the TV screen again in his boxers. She unlocked the door and walked in. The apartment was dark and empty. Impulsively, she put on every light in the house. It felt cold too. She put the heating on before having a look inside the kitchen. The case was still there. Tentatively, she shoved it aside. No marks or stains under it. No blood dripping out of the edges. Just the case resting in the middle of the floor. She couldn't even smell anything. It was a pity to open it back up. But she opened it anyway. She unzipped the case and flung the lid over. The smell hit her hard in the face. It smelled of a butcher's shop in a public rest-room. She looked at the towel that covered his face. She peeled it back:

His skin had lost every drop of colour, even his lips, even his under eye purple bags. It was paler than she had ever seen anyone. Even when people were very ill, they had some blood flow deep under the skin that made them look pinkish or grey. He looked like someone had stretched translucent white silk over something faintly blue and grey. There was no warmth to his colour at all. His hairs looked like they were drawn on his face and head with black marker. His lips had pulled back from his teeth and his eyelids had opened slightly, revealing not just the white, but some of the coloured iris and black pupil as well. His teeth and tongue, faintly visible between the stretched lips, looked bone dry.

Anna retched and ran to the bathroom, flinging herself over the edge of the toilet bowl where she heaved until she brought up yellow bile. Whatever had gone in that day was coming out. She dried her face with some tissue and flushed it. She would have to go back to the case. She would have to cover his face again and zip him up. She drew a deep breath and wandered into the kitchen again. Strangely, the smell was hardly present. She knelt down beside the case and reached for the towel.

"You know, I really wish you wouldn't do that." Jake said.

Anna froze, the towel slipping through her fingers and landing on his face.

"Oh great, more humiliation. As if sitting in a travel case in my own shit wasn't enough." Jake continued. The towel over his face didn't move and the voice wasn't muffled by the fabric.

Anna slowly lifted it off him again.

"That's better." Jake said as his now open eyes were revealed. The face didn't move.

"You're alive? Oh my God, I'm so sorry, I thought I'd killed you." Anna gasped, touching his face. It was ice cold.

"You did. Fucking idiot. Why would you shove someone in the kidneys before checking your hands?"

"I'm sorry, I- I... I'm going mad." Anna said to herself. She dragged the towel over Jake's face again, closed the case and made her way into the living room, where she curled up on the sofa. The silence was blissful, but short.

"You're not going mad, ya know? Well, you are, but you can't leave me here. I mean, I might not be alive, but I'm still your boyfriend.

Unless that whole knife to the guts thing was a breakup." His voice came through as loud and as clear as if he were sitting next to her.

"You're not real." She replied.

"Of course I am. Come back in. Have a look."

"No, *you're* not. The voice. It isn't real." Anna contested.

"I'm here, aren't I? Look, can we have this argument when I'm not sitting in my own shit? This isn't dignified, Anna. At least get me a shower, put me in some nice clothes and swap these plastics out before you lock me away."

She tried to ignore the voice as she made herself a microwave pizza for dinner and as she ate it, watching a soap, but it seemed the voice was louder than anything else she could hear. In the end, she finished half her dinner and went to bed.

"I'm still waiting Anna." The voice came from next to her. She rolled over in bed to face the usual empty space. "No, not in there. But come to think of it, you never did zip up the case..."

Anna gulped. "Leave me alone!"

"Look, I'm just joshing ya, if I could move I'd be in the shower by now. Come on sweetie, lend me a hand."

Anna sighed. "Will you let me sleep if I do?"

"Of course sweetie."

Getting up, she went into the kitchen. Sure enough, the case was unzipped. She zipped it back up and dragged it into the bathroom. She collected some more plastic bags to line the case and a bin bag to throw away the previous wrappings. Then she unzipped and unwrapped him. He was in a mess. The blood was drying and crackling all over him. There were feces all down his legs from where she had thrown his body around. Gross. She tried moving his body, but it proved impossible. His torso sat up in the case and rested against the side of the bath. She would have to get him in from inside the bath. She stripped off and got into the bath, dreading the feel of his cold, dead, stained body against hers. She grabbed him under the armpits and slowly heaved him in, slipping over and over. Once he was laying down in the bath, she put the hot shower head on and hosed his body down, again and again, with hot water until he looked clean enough to use a sponge on.

"Ah, that's better." Jake said. She had almost forgotten why she was going this.

"Please don't speak." She asked.

"Sorry sweetie."

The silence was almost as bad as him talking. She finished washing him down, packed the newly cleaned and dried towels around him to dry him and went to find some clothes. "I feel insane" She muttered as she took his favourite shirt and a pair of jeans into the bathroom.

"You are." Jake replied. "You know, all that time in a case has got me thinking... what about our holiday?"

"What about it?"

"Well, don't we still have the first tickets? Argentina for two?"

"I suppose." She said, struggling to wriggle the corpse into a shirt.

"And that's next month, right?"

"Yeah." Why was she still talking to a corpse? It felt strange. But she couldn't help but answer.

"Are we still going?"

Anna paused. "You're dead."

"But you could bring me. We could go together. Have a great time."

"You're dead." Anna repeated. She awkwardly finished forcing his jeans up and buttoned them before relining the case. It was easier to get him back into confinement when she had something solid to grip onto, though his arms were still awkwardly positioned. She forced them down hard with the case lid. There was a crack.

"Watch it!" Jake complained.

"A deal's a deal. It's bedtime." Anna left the case in the bathroom and went to bed. He left her alone to sleep. But she couldn't drift off.

Perhaps she should go on her trip to Argentina? Just not in a month. Tomorrow. And not for a few days. Forever. She could hop on a plane and disappear. It would be fine. Easy, even. And how would people track her if she actually went on her round the world trip? She could leave Jake here and all. Just pack up and go.

The next morning, she awoke to her alarm and turned it off before the volume went up. Today was a new day. She packed her bags with everything she would need. Four changes of clothes, make-up, hair products, shoes, some nice jewellery, money, passport. She logged online and booked a new ticket. She was pleased that she got a percentage off it for cancelling her old tickets.

"Aren't you forgetting someone?" Jake asked.

"You're back."

"I'll always be here." Jake replied.

Anna felt a chill run down her spine. "Even if I leave the case?"

"Even if you leave the case." He sounded almost smug.

"Can't I get away?"

"Not from me. But we can both get away together. I mean, think about it. I can't cheat on you now, can I? And no money worries for me. Our savings will take you twice as far and you could even retire in some Asian shithole with the money we have. Just bring me with you and we're together forever."

"That sounds convincing." Anna smiled. It did. It really did sound nice.

"Maybe me dying was the best thing to happen to us." Jake insisted.

"Maybe." Anna added extra carry on to her plane ticket.

"When are we leaving?" Jake asked.

"This afternoon. Train down to the airport, then straight to Argentina." Anna replied.

"That sounds awesome."

Anna rang work and told them that she and Jake were back together and heading to Argentina early, that she was quitting and wouldn't be back. There were a few tears, but mostly nobody cared. She called her friends and told them she would Skype as soon as they were there. She rang the landlord and explained she would leave the last month's payment on the table and the keys through the letterbox. She called a taxi and asked the driver to collect her bags.

The driver seemed apprehensive about the smell. Anna could hardly notice it herself, but the man almost gagged when he picked up Jake's case.

Anna shrugged. "I didn't have time to wash the laundry before going. Sorry."

The driver shook his head, dragged the luggage downstairs and threw the case in the back before slamming the boot shut.

"Ouch. Bastard." Jake muttered.

"Soon we'll be in Argentina." Anna smiled as she sat back in the passenger seat.

"We?" The driver asked.

"Uh, I'm meeting some folks there." Anna smiled some more.

"Uh-huh." The driver shook his head again and started the car.

Once they were there and unloaded, the taxi couldn't get away soon enough. He threw the cases down for Anna, got back in and drove off. He even forgot his payment. Anna shrugged. "All the more for us." She started dragging the cases along the station. Even on wheels, Jake weighed so much they wouldn't turn and they were grinding and squeaking as she hauled him across to the right end of the platform. One side faced the rails and on the other was a small wall overlooking an artificial lake. She wondered why it was there and how come there was so little protection between her and the water. It seemed ridiculous.

Looking around at her fellow passengers, they all seemed to be staring at her. She lifted her hand to scratch her head and realized she was still exactly as she had come out of bed. Suddenly she felt self-conscious, but there wasn't anything she could do now. And still, they stared...

She sat down on Jake's case and sighed. Well, at least they wouldn't live here much longer. That way she wouldn't be the weirdo in town. Who cared what these people thought?

But chills travelled down her spine when she spotted the police officer out of the corner of her eye. She knew that the woman with the caramel skin and the blue shirt was looking for her. She had to be. She was glancing up and down, marching decidedly towards that end of the platform. The policewoman *knew*.

"She knows." Jake said. "She knows what you did. She'll find the smell and find me and, well, who would believe you?"

Anna swallowed hard. Only one thing for it. She stood up and looked at the case.

"Anna? What are you doing?" Jake asked, sounding a bit nervous.

Anna began pushing the case towards the wall.

"You're only drawing attention to yourself sweetie." He pressed.

She turned the case on its side by the tiny wall. It would easily flip over.

"Shit, Anna, don't do this. Don't do this to me." The voice grew louder.

Anna glanced down the platform to see the officer start running towards her. She shoved the case into the artificial lake. At first it looked like it would get stuck on the concrete slope. But slowly it slid down, down, down into the water.

"You bitch." Jake said as the officer's hand seized Anna's arm.

"Is everything OK?" The officer asked.

Anna shook. "Yeah." Her eyes met the woman's. The officer wasn't impressed.

"You have to come with me sweetie." She said.

Anna felt repulsed at being called that by anyone but Jake. She stared longingly at the waters that had swallowed his body for good.

In the station, the officer asked Anna a few random questions. Who she was. Where she was going. Why was she going so suddenly. Why hadn't she got dressed in the morning. Anna answered as honestly as possible. She was Anna Mann. She was going to Argentina. She wanted a break. She had been a bit late. Jake's voice was gone and her mind felt so clear, so fresh and invigorated. Officer Terry Welsch nodded, smiled, took notes and went to make a phone call. It was all seeming to look like the officer would write it up to misunderstanding. If Anna could get away before they trenched out Jake's body, then... Then maybe...

"Sorry sweetie." She said, walking into the room. "We can't seem to find your bag."

Anna sighed and groaned. "Great, I'll have to go clothes shopping in Argentina."

"We could *all* do with some clothes shopping." Terry sighed. "Speaking of which, it's warm in here." She undid the very top button of her tight blue shirt, revealing more caramel skin and a necklace. A necklace Anna would have recognized anywhere.

Terry followed Anna's eye-line. "Oh yeah, my boyfriend gave it to me. Said his mother made him wear it for some charity thing. Well, I should say ex boyfriend. Fucker stood me up last night. Sort of like yours." Terry laughed. "I guess I should throw it, only... I don't know, I kinda like it." She shrugged and turned, walking to the door where she started fiddling with the AC. "I swear, it's awful in here. Maybe it's broke again..."

Anna glanced down at the table. The only thing on it was a pen. But she'd seen in a film that a pen, driven through an eye or an ear with enough force, could easily kill...

SHIT HOLE

MARY SAVAGE

Chapter One

He'd spent five years in that hellhole before he made an informed decision: prison fucking sucks. He spent the majority of his day locked in a cell with some psychopath that claimed to hear voices in his head telling him to do crazy shit like wear his underwear on his head or punch that big guy, Stone, in the yard. Stone had nearly killed the poor bastard, but Joe Sullivan, aka "Sully" here, didn't give two shits about him. Not when he ate something gray that might have once been meat for breakfast, lunch, *and* dinner and drank water with a yellowish tint to it. Not when he slept on mattresses lumpier than the alley floors he used to sleep on as a kid, when his mother was jobless and they had no place to call home. Not when he had these assholes who call themselves correctional officers screaming in his ear like they're talking to some old deaf guy and shoving him around like it's some kind of game.

So many times he's wanted to retaliate, to bash their heads in, to slit their throats with a handmade shank, to slap their own cuffs onto their wrists and beat them mercilessly with their own nightsticks. But he was smarter than that; he knew that were he to so much as pluck a single hair from any guard's head, there would be consequences. Namely, more time added on to his sentence and even harsher punishment from the dickheads within the prison itself; the very same ones that were supposed to be protecting him from his other cell mates.

But the very worst part about all of this shit was the fact that he hadn't even done anything wrong to deserve it—well, at least not what they *thought* he'd done.

He's not going to lie; he's wasted a few traitors to the gang. More than one man is buried six feet under with his trademark cigarette burn on the back of the neck, but he swears on his mother's grave that he never even went near that chick they're saying he offed. He didn't even recognize her name, but apparently she was some rich bitch daughter of a senator or something. Raped and killed and dumped in an alley about a mile away from his house, a cigarette burn on the back of her neck and a threatening letter—supposedly from him—found in the pocket of her designer coat.

The police had barely even had to prove his guilt. He was so well-known in this city, by all the jurors and the deliberation had taken less than a minute before he was found Guilty of all crimes. He was sentenced to 20-Life and sent upstream. His girl, Pat, visited him sometimes and they used Morse taps to communicate as they chatted about mundane subjects like the weather and sports games he couldn't give two shits about.

Through their taps, he found out about the man who framed him, Rick Silas, who'd once been his friend, but was now a bitter rival. Rick and Joe had had a falling out years ago over something as absurd as splitting their shares from a lifted purse. There was only about a hundred dollars in the damn thing and Rick's argument was that, since he's the one who distracted the old lady in the first place, he should get a bigger split. Joe fought that it should be equal, since they both did their part in the theft. They'd fought like animals afterwards and one sock in the jaw had Rick backing off.

"Keep it, you greedy fuck!" he roared. "I'll find my own!" It had been a year until he saw Rick again and by that time he already had his own operation going. And Rick was never one to let go of grudges easily.

Cops starting inexplicably hanging around Joe's house, where he, Pat, and their own group of 'outlaws' lived. They sold drugs, stole drugs, used persuasive tactics—such as wielding a knife or a gun—to get their own way, and sold knockoffs. With the cops watching their place, Joe had to be ten times as careful, warding off the fuzz with his natural charm and power of persuasion. He fucked more than one female cop while Pat gave blowjobs to the majority of the males. They weren't bothered at all until the rich bitch turned up dead.

When the cops came to his door then, they didn't even ask questions before shoving a warrant in his face and slapping cuffs on him. At the time, Joe had no idea what he'd done or who had accused him but he already swore revenge as they shoved him into the back of a police car. Nobody wanted to listen to him plead his innocence and his trial was set for the following month, at the senator's insistence.

To find out that it was Rick was no big surprise, but he cursed out loud nonetheless, causing two of the guards to look his way.

"It's supposed to rain tomorrow," he lied and they looked away, uncaring.

It was then that he started to plan his revenge, meeting with Pat every few weeks to tap it out. She informed them that half of their guys had gone over to Rick's side when Joe went away, that they were now loyal to him and they were missing half of their manpower. Nobody had discovered the drug ring, but people were wary about buying from them now that their leader was away. Rick had done all of this, the prick. He would pay.

Now it was five years later and still there was no way to put their plan into action without Joe there to guide them. Pat was persuasive, but she was no gang leader, that was for damn sure. She was just his right hand; the person who echoed his orders and pointed a gun at whoever wavered. She was loyal and tough, but not tough enough for what he had in mind.

He was being driven insane every single day as he listened to his roommate mutter to himself, his head banging a rhythm against the wall. The only thing that kept him going anymore was the thirst for revenge. And Ann's letters.

Ann was another rich bitch. But she hadn't known the victim too well, except for the rumors she heard about the girl's tryst with some gang member. She was the first to write to him and tell him that she believed he was innocent. She wrote, in her first letter, that the gang member the girl was associated with was black, not white like Joe, and lived on the other side of the city—at least according to the rumors she'd heard. She'd tried to tell the cops that but none of them had listened. As far as they were concerned, she was just another little heiress looking for attention.

But the fact that somebody outside his own group thought he was innocent was enough to make Joe respond to that first letter—and then every letter thereafter. Their correspondence lasted for the entirety of his time in prison and he kept every single letter in his pillowcase, smiled when they crinkled at night as he rolled over. He didn't tell Pat about the letters.

He received one on the day his plans would be set into motion.

"Dear Joe,

Since receiving your last letter, I've been thinking a lot about what I would like to do for the rest of my life and I've decided that I'm going to go for it. I'm going to tell my father about my art, show him my paintings. Maybe he'll understand, you know? Maybe he won't be mad at all. I mean, I'm his daughter and he loves me, doesn't he? Won't he just be happy that I'm happy? I'm sure he will and so I'm going to tell him. Better late than never, after all. Right?

And Joe, I don't think I've ever asked you want you want to be. As in your career? I know it'll be a while before you can even consider it, but what is it that you've always wanted to do with your life? Something besides a life of crime, I mean, though to each his own I guess. Let me know in your next letter. I'll be looking forward to it.

Sincerely, Ann Martin"

It was shorter than most of his letters but he tucked it away into the inner coat of his jacket anyway. He would answer no more letters but he wouldn't leave them here, where psycho could get his hands on them. And, besides, having them closer to him made him feel safer as he made his way into the yard, where hundreds of other inmates stood, talking and just taking in the short amount of fresh air they were allotted each day.

Joe strolled casually through the crowds, down a familiar trail, his eyes skating over the faces of guards and his fellow inmates, many of whom were watching him. Platt, a lifer whose cell was located three down from Joe's gave him a hard glance and Joe smirked, held up two fingers, and walked further down the path, approaching the fence. He stopped and sat on the ground, closing his eyes as he counted backwards from a hundred and twenty. At five, his eyes opened again, just in time to see Platt punch Linster in the jaw. This was followed by Brown, another inmate, who sat with Joe at most meals, kneeing some unknown Latino in the groin.

Joe watched as the entire yard dissolved into chaos. The guards all around the yard ran straight towards the mess of inmates fighting one another, throwing punches and kicks and attacking one another with clawed hands. He smiled and reveled in the beauty of it before turning on his head and continuing down the path. Nobody even looked his way.

At the edge of the yard, about a quarter mile away from the entrance into the prison, there was a weak spot of fence. It wasn't electric, for safety reasons, but barbed wire ran all over its length and height—except here. Here, there was a noticeable gap in the barbs, where they split and were easily moved away to reveal a hole in the fence itself. When Joe had first noticed it, after taking a few laps around the sparse yard, there had been no way he could fit through it. It was too small even for the slender Pat to fit through.

But five years, fifty pounds less, and a bit of digging with a hundred or so easily broken plastic spoons, and the hole he made just underneath it might allow him a not-so-easy exit. This was his only chance at escape, either way. He had traded all his belongings to Platt and Brown for their little stunt. Platt didn't take too much convincing but Brown wasn't a lifer and had demanded almost more than Joe could give.

It proved worth it when Joe got down on his knees and slid through the hole like a slithering snake. Maybe he'd lost more weight than he thought in that shithole. He'd have to find a way to make it back after he got settled and wasted that dirtbag of an ex-partner, Rick.

He stood, brushed himself off, and then ran, never looking over his shoulder. The street was just a few hundred yards away and Pat would be waiting for him there, her trunk already open for him to jump into, a bag of fresh clothes for him to change into. She always had him covered, his Pat.

By the time he reached the car, he figured they must be looking for him so he wasted no breath to say hello or thank her for what she was doing. He just jumped into the trunk, shut it, and rolled around as she drove off. But he didn't really care about how sore his muscles were or what a close call he might have just had because he was free.

He was finally fucking free.

Chapter Two

There was absolutely no way they could return to his old house. For one thing, that would have been the first place they looked for him, and for another...well, since his incarceration and the whole operation going belly up and everything, they'd been forced to sell it.

"We got everything out, though," she told him as they walked into the new safe house, located about twenty miles from the city, in the middle of a large wooded area. It had belonged to Pat's late father, used only for fishing and cheating on her mother with his skanks. "It's all here, in the basement. The boys are out on the streets with it right now."

"How do they get back and forth?" Joe asked, always worried about his boys. He tugged his jeans up his hips; they were too big for him now.

"I drive them," Pat told him. "And Jimmy's got a good car now, too."

"Jimmy's sixteen," Joe snorted, looking around the tiny, damp living room.

"Not anymore," Pat said, tugging his hand as she moved towards the couch. "He's got a girl and a kid now. He's got a job down at the docks."

"And he's still selling?"

"He's still loyal. Besides, he ain't making enough to support his family with that dock shit; he needs the cash so I try to help him out, you know." Pat pushed him down onto the couch and climbed up onto his lap, smiling down on him like the Cheshire cat. "Let's not talk about it now, though, alright? We got more important things to do." She began to press kisses against his neck, smiling against his skin as he planted his hands on her hips.

"Pat, babe, we shouldn't—" he started but she pulled back and placed one finger against his lips to silence him.

"We've got plenty of time to do other shit, Joey," she said, "but you've been locked up for half a decade; surely there's something you missed in that time, huh? A bit more, uh, *pressing* issue." She palmed him and he groaned. "See? Now just sit back and relax; Patti's got it all covered, baby."

He was too distracted to argue further.

They lay in bed after three full rounds of what could barely be called sex. It was more like Pat had pounced on him, doing 90% of the work while he just lay there, reaping the benefits. The bed in the master bedroom was ten times as comfortable as the old prison mattress and he found himself starting to drift off as Pat lay against him, catching him up on everything that had happened since their last prison visit.

"...and he got that Martin girl all tied up somewhere in his house. Also, Jimmy's girl is pregnant again with a—"

"Wait," Joe interrupted. "What did you say? About the Martin girl? You mean *Ann*?"

"Yah, I think that's 'er name. Why? You know her?" Pat asked, looking up at him.

Joe nodded as he sat up, dislodging Pat. "Yeah," he said. "she, ah, wrote to me. In prison."

"She's one of *those* chicks?" Pat laughed. "Crazy ass women fallin' for convicts who'd sooner kill them than—"

"You sayin' I'm a murderer, Pat?" Joe barked, startling her.

"'Course not, Joey," she assured him. "I mean, I know you killed people, but those bastards always had it comin', didn't they? So it's all good. I'm just saying *she* didn't know that, is all."

Joe took a deep breath and rubbed the back of his neck. "I know what you're sayin'," he said. "But Ann didn't think I was guilty. She said I must've been framed 'cause I didn't match the description of the girl's boyfriend. Apparently, he was in a gang too."

"Did she say which?" Ann asked, sitting up to rest on her knees next to him.

Joe nodded. "It was Rick's, obviously," he said. "We know that. Poor girl was probably lured in and murdered in cold blood."

"Not before they got their way with her I'll bet," Pat huffed. "Poor...what was her name again?"

"Something Grant, I don't fuckin' know," Joe sighed. "Point is, he killed that poor girl just to get back at me and now he's gonna kill Ann, too. 'Less we do somethin' about it."

"Which we are," Pat reminded him. "In just a few short weeks, we're gonna infiltrate his place and—"

"We don't have weeks, Patti," Joey growled, throwing the sheets off of his legs and standing. He grabbed his boxers and began pulling his clothes on. "We don't even have a few days. You know Rick; he'll play with his new little toy for a few days and then he'll get bored, shoot her dead, and bury her in the backyard." He shook his head. "I've seen him do it too many times and I ain't about to let another girl die on my account."

"So what do you wanna do, then?" Pat asked, following him out of the room, a sheet wrapped around her naked body. "Just storm in there with no backup *tonight*? He's got a million guys in that house of his; ain't no way we're gonna take them all down, just the two of us."

"He won't be keeping her in his house, anyway," Joe dismissed. "He's too smart for that. 'Specially since that girl's daddy is probably lookin' everywhere for her right at this very moment. No, he's keepin' her somewhere, but wh—" His eyes widened as he looked back at Pat. "Is Sabretooth still around?"

"You mean Rick's bitch?" Pat snorted humorlessly, shaking her head, dirty blonde locks shaking with the motion. "'Course he is. But you don't think..." Joe grinned. "Rick wouldn't keep that girl with Sabe; he's a twice-convicted rapist. He couldn't expect the perv to resist somebody like that."

"You said it yourself; Sabretooth is Rick's bitch; whatever he says, that dumbass does. Rick probably distracted him with a couple dozen of his own hoes, anyhow." He paused to take a breath. "Where's he livin' now, Sabretooth. He still got that house on Seventh?"

"Far as I know," Pat said. "I haven't spoken to the bastard in years, but I don't really see any reason for him to change his address; he's been out of jail eight years now. Supposedly, he's doing good, despite more allegations coming up on the contrary." She shook her head. "Even if Sabe *does* have the Martin girl, do you know how hard it's gonna be to bring down all *his* goons? We're gonna need at least a half dozen of our guys and I don't think they'll be up for something like that tonight, babe."

"First light, then," Joe said. "We'll leave when the sun rises; make sure everybody's got their shit together."

"Sweetheart," Pat replied, "I'm loyal to you; you know I am. But I ain't no miracle worker and those boys haven't had their shit together since they was in diapers."

Chapter Three

By morning, all but three of Joe's main group of men had arrived back to Pat's safehouse. Jimmy, Sam, and Teddy were all family men now, which surprised Joe but he wasn't about to take them away from what they'd all worked so hard to gain.

Besides, even without them he still had more than a dozen guys ready to help him take Sabretooth down. Sabe had been one of them once, before Rick had betrayed them all. It hadn't taken the bastard a week to pack up all his shit and run to Rick's side, though. Joe hadn't even been surprised—nor did he care, considering Sabretooth was a lousy shot and proved to be a double-crosser, anyway. Who needed him?

Thankfully, all the men that stayed knew Sabe well enough to know all his tells and his strengths and weaknesses and how fucking dumb that man got when anything in a skirt showed up. He thought with his dick and that was a fatal flaw that made Joe burst into random bouts of laughter. His boys followed.

The plan was simple: Their three strongest—Bo, Gabe, and Devon—would lead the group. Being the muscle meant that they'd be able to easily take out any shitheads guarding around the house and allow the rest to get in. Behind them were about six of Joe's most weapon-savvy men; TJ, Mart, Steve, Bardy, Paulie, and Fisher. Their weapons were, for the most part, concealed by their clothing, but easily accessible when they needed them. They would enter the house before Pat, Joe, and the rest, guns blazing as they took out anyone on the first floor (though they were warned to be way of any blonde girls who looked as if they might be scared or mistreated.) Once they cleared, Joe and Pat would lead the others upstairs, where Ann was most likely be held. He knew, from experience, that there were only three possible rooms she could be held in, so they would be split into partners. He and Pat would be together, of course.

"This girl really that important to you?" Dove, the only other female gang member asked as they waited for the all-clear from Bardy. "I wouldn't even go that far for a piece of ass."

"She ain't a piece of ass, Dove," Joe snapped. "She's an innocent. And the only person who believed me when she didn't have to. We don't let people like that die on our watch, alright?"

"Okay, okay," Dove muttered. "Damn."

"Clear!" Bardy called out to Joe and he lead them out from the gathering of bushes they'd been hiding in, each pulling out their weapons as they approached the house. Joe took the safety off his Glock as he immediately started up the stairs. Pat was on his heel. At the top of the stairs, they split into their groups. Dove went with Stu, and Bardy would search another room with TJ, while Pat and Joe took the last room.

"You ready for this?" Pat asked him. "You might not like what you see. She might already be dead."

"I'll hate myself if I don't make sure," Joe responded. "So, yes. I'm ready."

"Fingers crossed." Pat kicked in the door, her gun pointed inside.

The room was completely empty, but for a few chairs and boxes, and three people. The first was the man himself; Sabretooth was a slimy man with a shark's tooth necklace around his neck. He was skinny and tall and his breath constantly stank of onions. It was no wonder he had to stoop as low as rape to get any action. Just the very sight of him made Joe's stomach lurch; he was sickening.

Behind him was a scantily clad, brown-skinned woman with firetruck-red short hair that hung over her eyes in a fringe. She barely even glanced their way, too distracted by the tiny blonde she had her arms wrapped around, her lips attached to the pulse point of a visibly uncomfortable young woman.

Ann. That was Joe's Ann. The same woman who's scrawling cursive he'd read at least twice a week since he was sent away. Her dress was torn and her makeup was smudged and her hair looked like a rat's nest, but there was no mistaking the woman in all the pictures she'd sent him over the years. Only the woman in the pictures was constantly smiling; there was no trace of a smile on her face her. Not even when he could clearly read the look recognition on her face. Instead, he looked absolutely terrified.

"What did you do to her?" Joe barked at Sabe, who just grinned in return.

"Hey to you, too, Joey; how've you been?" he responded. "How was prison?"

"What did you do to her?" Joe repeated, completely ignoring the other man's questions.

"Me?" Sabe asked, as if offended. "Absolutely nothing. My girl, Lourdes, however..."

"GET YOUR HANDS OFF OF HER!" Joe boomed, his gun pointing in the woman's direction. She didn't even blink.

"Don't be ridiculous," Sabretooth laughed. "She knows you won't do anything while she'd wrapped around your girl. Lourdes may be a hoe, but she ain't stupid." He laughed again and pulled his own gun. "I, however, don't care about either bitch." He pointed his gun at them and finally Lourdes stopped, her eyes going wide.

"Sabe?" she asked, stepping away from Ann, who fell to the floor in a fit of sobs. Sabretooth wasted no time in shooting her through the school. Lourdes's body fell to the floor as blood gushed from the wound in her head and Ann screamed. Sabretooth pointed the gun at her next and she began to beg and plead for her life.

"He won't hurt you," Joe told her. "He can't."

"The fuck you mean, I can't?" Sabretooth hissed, his gun trained on Ann's head. "You've seen me shoot bitches before, haven't you? Or have you forgotten?"

"I haven't forgotten what a little bitch you are," Joe said, taking a step forward. Sabe's gun swung around to point at him.

"The fuck you say to me?" he growled. "I ain't no bitch."

Joe scoffed. "Of course you are," he said. "You were my bitch for years and then you left me to be Rick's bitch. And no bitch of Rick's is about to kill his favorite toy; not if he don't wanna be killed in return. Trust me, Sabe, you're a total bitch."

"You wanna see a bitch, motherfucker?" Sabretooth growled. "Why do you watch me waste *yours*?" His head started to swing back but before it could, Ann's hand slapped down on it, forcing the gun out of his grip. It clattered across the floor and she immediately jumped after it. So did Sabretooth, but before he could pull the blonde back, Pat shot his leg and he cried out in pain. "BITCH!" he bellowed.

"You know it," Pat replied, blowing on the muzzle of her gun, before re-holstering it. Ann was able to grab the gun and stood, pointing it down at Sabretooth, who was immobilized by the pain in his leg but looked up at the shaky weapon with defiance.

"What are you gonna do, bitch?" he asked. "Shoot me? You don't got the balls."

Ann glared at him but her hands continued to shake. She took a step back and Sabe laughed. Pat shook her head and glanced up at Joe. "You want me to waste him?" she asked.

"No," Joe said, his eyes trained on Ann. "Let her do it." Ann looked up at that and her eyes pleaded with him. She shook her head. "It's alright," he said. "Think about all the horrible things he did to you. Think about what he did to Lourdes, his own girl. He was about to do the same to you. He deserves this, alright? Nobody would blame you for offin' him. And, trust me, it feels so fuckin' good to do an asshole like that in, to give him what he deserves. Just go ahead and you'll see. Trust me, Ann. Do you trust me?" Ann nodded, but continued to waver. "You'll be okay."

She nodded again and pulled the trigger. The sound the gun made was deafening in the silence of the room. Sabretooth's body went limp after the bullet lodged in his cranium and blood splattered over the floor and Ann's bare feet. The gun dropped from her shaky hand to the ground and her knees began to wobble. She looked to Joe for help and he stepped forward, catching her in his arms before she could reach the floor.

"I've got you," he whispered against her hair. "I've got you, Ann." She buried her face into his chest and began to sob as he rubbed her back.

Pat watched with undisguised hurt, but Joe didn't notice. She took a deep breath and swallowed past the lump in her throat, turning to the other men. "Come on," she said, "we don't wanna be around when the fuzz shows up." She stormed past the confused group, not even sparing Joe and Ann a glance over her shoulder to see that he'd lifted the woman into his arms and was now carrying her, bridal-style, out of the room.

Joe's eyes remained focused on Ann the whole time. "I'm gonna get you outta here, okay?" he whispered in her ear. "You'll be okay. Gonna get you somewhere nice and safe, alright?"

"Okay," Ann sniffed against his shirt, her arms tight around his neck already.

It was in that moment that Ann Martin realized how deeply and fathomlessly in love she was with Joe Sullivan.

Chapter Four

It took them less than 24 hours to get Ann cleaned up, patched up, buy her some new clothes, feed her, and purchase her a train ticket to Stamford, CT. Her family lived in Manhattan, but Joe figured it would be too easy for anybody to snatch her here in the city. At least in Connecticut she would be safe with Pat's cousin, Carly.

"Now, listen," he told her once they made it to Grand Central, "Carly's gonna meet you at the platform. Don't be stupid and go wandering off alone, okay? Somebody might come after you and you don't want to be alone when that happens. Carly's tough and protective as all hell; she's the one that's gonna keep you safe in our absence."

"But, Joe, I—" Ann started to argue.

"No," Joe cut her off, shaking his head. "No arguments right now, okay? We're trying to save your life and this is the best way to do it, okay?" Ann nodded, tears in her eyes. "Okay. Now, as soon as we've got everything settled over here, either me or Pat is gonna come get you in Stamford. We'll call Carly first to let you know we're on our way, okay?" Ann nodded and Joe gave her a gentle smile. "You're gonna be okay, kid," he said, cupping her cheek with one hand. "Everything's gonna be okay now." Ann took a deep breath and canted into him, wrapping her arms around his neck and pressing her face into his neck.

"Don't die," she whispered, on a shuddery breath. She pulled back. "Promise me you won't die." Her gaze was steely and Joe couldn't help but nod at that.

"I promise," he said and she smiled sadly up at him, leaning up on her toes to press her lips against his. Joe returned her kiss, his hands cupping her slender hips. Pat watched from the side with a frown, before looking away.

"Better wrap it up," she said, suddenly, looking at her watch. "The train is leaving in about ten minutes." Joe and Ann pulled apart, sighing. Tears streamed down Ann's cheeks and Joe brushed them away with his thumbs.

"Everything will be alright," he said again. "You'll see. Now, go." He backed away from her and Ann took a deep breath, grabbing her bag and heading in the direction of her platform. Before she reached it, she looked back and locked eyes with Joe. She gave him one last wave and blew him a kiss and he offered her a weak smile in return.

When she was gone, Joe's smile disappeared and he turned to Pat. "Let's go get this asshole," he practically growled, starting towards the exit. Pat was right on his heels.

Infiltrating Rick's brownstone was a much harder feet than they'd originally thought. He lived on a more populated street, so the outdoor guards were not an option. That was good in some ways, Joe thought, but now they had no idea exactly how many people were actually *inside* the damn building because every single window was blocked by thick curtains. And in the daytime, there would be no lights on to give even a shadow so they were going in completely blind.

"Listen," Joe said as they planned it all out. "We may lose a few good men today. But I want you all to know how glad I am to have you all on my side. You've remained loyal to me for all these years and I'm grateful for that. Each one of you has a place in my heart."

"Did prison turn you into a sap, Sullivan?" Bardy growled out, making the others laugh. "'Cause I thought it was supposed to make you tougher."

"Looks like it had the opposite effect," TJ piped in, making them all laugh again.

"Fuck you all," Joe laughed, shaking his head. "Alright," he said, "let's get on with it. If anybody finds that bastard before me, keep him alive; I wanna be the one to put that bullet through his skull, got it?" They nodded and broke apart.

Trying to appear inconspicuous, they split into groups, their weapons concealed by clothing and bags. Dove and Pat linked arms like girlfriends and pretended to gossip about their boyfriends, strutting down the street in tight dresses and heels. One group of their men pretended to whistle at them as they passed; another group was dressed as businessmen and carried their weapons in briefcases. Joe had on a hoodie and a pair of headphones in his ears that weren't actually connected to anything. Nobody noticed that they were headed in the exact same direction.

There was an alley in between Rick's brownstone and the one next to it, which they all slipped into, one group at a time. From there, Joe was able to get a good look at the back of the building, through the slats of a broken fence. "There's a fire escape leading into the yard," he told Pat. "We could probably climb it while the others start from the first floor; corner him, ya know?"

Pat nodded. "Good plan," she said. "But there's one leading out the front, too."

"You take one," Joe said, "I'll take the other." It wasn't too complicated.

"What if he's not alone?"

Joe groaned. "TJ, go with Pat; Bardy, come with me." The men nodded. "All the rest, start from the bottom and make your way up. From the looks of it, we've got three floors to deal with here. Make sure Rick gets to the third floor and, remember, don't kill the bastard. I'll handle that part."

There were murmurs of agreement as everybody got into position. Pat and TJ went around the front and climbed up the fire escape, careful not to pass clear in front of a window, lest they give themselves away. Nobody from the street even glanced their way.

Joe and Bardy situated themselves on the back fire escape while the rest of their team waited at every possible entrance for a sign from them to begin.

"Everybody in position?" Joe whispered in his walkie talkie. There was a static of yeses coming from each individual talkie and he took a deep breath. "Okay. Go!" The sound of windows breaking, doors slamming open, shouts and growls and gunfire coming from inside. Joe and Bardy waited for the signal from Dove, telling them that it was safe to enter.

Ann Martin didn't get on the train. She couldn't. Not when she knew that Joe's life was in danger; not when she just recently realized how she felt about him. She just couldn't do it.

So she stood on the platform for fifteen minutes, waved stupidly to the train as it pulled out of the station, and then walked off the platform. She was almost relieved to see that Joe and Pat were no longer standing in the middle of Grand Central when she arrived, surrounded by a thousand other people desperately trying to find their own platforms. Tourists took pictures of the big clock and the constellations painted on the ceilings. They took in everything with wide eyes and even wider mouths, like this train station was something exceedingly special.

Ann had lived here for the whole of her life and she knew that there was absolutely nothing special about this place once you've seen for the hundredth time. Her parents had taken her through here so many times on their way to and from Westchester County, where they had an estate in Purchase, that it wore off by the time she was five. The train station, which had once been a colorful world full of excitement and adventure for a toddler, was now just...loud.

Ann hastened towards the exit as quickly as possible and breathed in the stale New York City air with reverence. She'd almost died just one day before and she never felt so grateful for the chance to breath in the smoky, polluted air of the city, to hear the thundering stutters of construction just down the street. To experience the hateful scowl on a native's face as they bumped into her on the sidewalk. She felt as if she were experiencing New York for the very first time.

Dragging her rolling suitcase behind her, she started in the direction of Washington Square Park. It would take her a while to get there, she knew that, but maybe she could...

Ann paused. What could she do? She didn't have any guns and she knew nothing she could say to Joe would help. He was intent on his revenge, intent on killing another man no matter what the consequences, and she knew that. Knew that he wouldn't stop until he achieved his goal. He would gladly go back to prison if it meant Rick Silas was dead on the ground.

But Ann couldn't let that happen. She couldn't lose him again, not like this. And any other way than Joe killing Rick meant that Rick killed Joe and she couldn't live with that knowledge either. So, no matter how long the distance, or how high the stakes, Ann would have to go after her love. She had to stop him, even if she risked her own life in the process.

He was completely worth it. At least in her mind. She just hoped that she wasn't too late.

"We lost Paulie!" Fisher's voice crackled through the walkie. Joe cursed and shared a look with Bardy, who'd practically been Paulie's guardian since the day he joined, a gangly kid of about 15, desperate to prove himself. Bardy had made him the weapons master he was now. Or had been.

"Sorry, man," Joe whispered. Bardy shook his head, his eyes filled with undisguised rage.

"He's gonna fuckin' pay for that," he growled in a low voice. Joe nodded, solemnly. His walkie crackled again.

"WE'VE GOT HIM!" Mart shouted through the line. "He's headed toward the third floor. Patti! Joey! Do you read me?!"

"Got it!" Pat's voice called and Joe could hear her without the damn talkie. "I'm goin' in!"

"Me too," Joe growled into the machine as he and Bardy readied their guns and stepped up to the window. "

"You ready for this?" Bardy asked in his low, rumbling voice.

Joe nodded. "As I'll ever be," he replied, taking a deep breath. Bardy nodded in return and they both turned to face the window. Joe held up one hand and started a slow countdown on it.

Three....two.....one!

They burst through the window, spilling glass into the room with them. They stumbled slightly at their entrance, but then held their guns up high, pointing them around the room.

It was small and crowded with bedroom furniture; a bed, a chest of drawers, an old vanity table and matching wooden bookcase. The window was next to the door and in the next second a familiar face appeared in the doorway, his hands held up over his head, a smug smile on his face.

"Rick Silas," Joe growled, then spit at the man's feet as they walked past. "Long time, no see."

Rick's head turned in their direction, hands staying up as Pat entered the room after him, her gun pointed at Rick's head. He smirked at the sight of his old foe. "Joseph Sullivan," he greeted. "I thought you were locked up."

"Got out early," Joe replied, his teeth gritted. "Good behavior and all that."

Rick snorted. "Good behavior? You?" He laughed a big, honking laugh. "Right. Ain't nobody gonna get out of jail for 'good behavior' when a senator's daughter gets off; least of all, you." He shook his head. "So how's you get out then?"

"Not really important," Joe replied, his gun still raised. "I'm out now, ain't I? Why dwell on the past?"

"Joey Sullivan," Rick sighed, "always thinking of the future; almost as much as you think of yourself, you greedy bastard."

"At least I'm not some whiny little bitch," Joe said. "So focused on getting my revenge that I put the lives of others at risk."

"That isn't what you're doing right now?" Rick retorted, his eyes skating over the injured men and women behind Joe's back.

"These are all *willing* participants," Joe informed him. "I didn't kill an innocent just to make a point. I'm no pussy when it comes to revenge, Silas. Not like you."

"Nobody's innocent," Rick said, smartly, his hands finally lowering. "You taught me that." He reached for his pocket and they all took a step forward. He put one hand back up. "Relax," he said, pulling out a butane lighter. He flicked it open, then closed. "Nervous habit," he explained, calmly, that smirk never leaving his face. Joe watched him calculatingly, before his eyes began to roam around the room.

For the first time since they burst in, he realized why there had been such opaque curtains hanging in every single window. On every surface, including the floor itself, there were candles; most lit, but some blown out, though wisps of smoke still rose from their wicks as if they'd been lit recently. It was no surprise, really, considering that Rick was a pyromaniac. He always had a lighter handy and enjoyed watching the wax melt on his candles. His weapon of choice was an impromptu flamethrower made from a can of hairspray and whatever lighter he typically had handy at the given moment.

His favorite had a picture of the Tasmanian Devil on it. More than once, Joe had joked that Taz was like the animated incarnation of Rick himself; crazy and unpredictable and incredibly volatile. Rick apparently still favored the character as Joe could just make out the little brown blob on the otherwise silver piece of metal. Some things never changed, he thought, as he continued to glare at the other man.

"I can't believe you still have that damn thing," Joe said, surprising himself even. He hadn't meant to start a conversation.

"My loyalty to Taz hasn't changed," Rick replied, still flicking the lid of his lighter open and close.

"At least you remained loyal to him," Joe retorted on a growl. "At least you remained loyal to *somebody.*"

"Still sore about that, are you?" Rick asked, grinning. "I wish you'd just let it go, man. We weren't *that* close."

"I couldn't give a shit less about your little betrayal," Joe informed him. "But what you did *after* that; killing that girl, sending me to prison to *rot* for five fucking years...you had it coming."

"Had what coming?" Rick asked, still smiling as if he didn't know. Joe cocked his gun in response and Rick's grin widened. "Oh," he said. "That." He took a calm breath and shook his head. "You're not *really* going to kill your best chance at going free, are you?" He flicked the lighter open. "The only person who can confirm that you didn't kill that poor Grant girl." He flicked it closed. "Think about it, Joey; if I'm gone, you're just going to go back to prison." Open.

"Not necessarily," Joe countered.

"What else then? You gonna go on the run?" He tilted his head, his eyes shining with amusement. "With your girl, Pat?" Joe's gun wavered and his mouth tightened. "No..." Rick continued with a titter. "That Martin girl? What's her name?" Joe refused to answer but his hand tightened around the gun. "Ann, right?" Joe still did not respond; he didn't have to. "Ann," Rick decided. "How is she? Still smarting from making her first kill?" Joe's eyes widened.

"How did you know about that?" he barked. Rick didn't even blink.

"You still think I don't have eyes everywhere, don't you?" Rick tutted. "Joey, Joey, Joey…when are you gonna learn? I see *everything*," he whispered, his grin becoming catlike.

"See this, punk!" Pat cried as she took a shot. Joe, at the last minute, shoved her arm, causing her bullet to fly at the hand holding Rick's lighter, which dropped on impulse as the man cursed.

"Fucking bitch!" he screamed as he held his hand to his chest. It was bleeding profusely. Joe glared at Pat.

"What did I fucking say?" he growled. She had the decency to look ashamed.

"Sorry," she grumbled. When he turned back to Rick, he was still holding his bleeding hand. And still cursing. "But he deserved it."

"That don't fucking matter," Joe growled at her. "You don't fucking dis—"

"FIRE!" Bardy screamed from behind them. Pat and Joe looked in the direction he was pointing and did, in fact, see a fire begin to bloom from the curtain, where Rick's lit lighter had fallen.

"Shit!" Joe barked, alerting Rick, who turned and let out a string of curses, starting in the direction of the door. Nearly a dozen weapons rose automatically, pointed straight at his head. He paused, turned and ran for the window—the one without the fire escape. He threw aside the curtain and jumped out while everybody watched in shock.

"Did he just fuckin'—" Pat asked.

"Yes," Bardy growled. "Yes, he did."

Joe wasn't convinced. He ran to the window, even as the flames grew around him.

"Joey!" Pat cried. "What the fuck are you doing? We gotta get outta this fuckin' place before it burns to the ground!"

"Go on!" Joe yelled back. "I need to make sure this sonofabitch is dead! I'll take the fire escape."

The others began to run out, some taking the fire escape while other hightailed it down the stairs. "I ain't leavin' you!" Pat cried, even as Dove started to pull her out. Bardy was urging her towards the fire escape, but she wouldn't go.

Joe ignored her, looking out the window. A sadistic grin spread over his features as he spotted Rick's crumpled body in the grass, joints bent at odd angles. He winced once in sympathy and shook his head, backing away from the window.

The room was now engulfed in flames. Those who had rushed to escape had inadvertently knocked over several candles, which only added to the overall fire. The breathable air was diminishing. Pat still stood at the window, hesitant to leave without him. Bardy was tugging on her arm, trying to get her to leave. She refused, pleading with Joe.

He nodded and started after her, before doubling back. He found the lighter next to the lit up curtains and grabbed it: his trophy. He closed it and tucked it deep into his pocket, before turning on his heel and running towards the fire escape.

He'd barely made it with the curtains of those windows burst into flames too, forcing him back. Pat jumped back as well and Bardy attempted to pick her up, but she struggled too much for him to get a good grip.

"We have to go!" he yelled.

"No!" Pat fought. "I won't leave without him!"

"Pat, go!" Joe ordered. "Get out of here!"

"No!" Pat screamed. "Not until I know you're safe!"

"I've got a plan," Joe called back, before turning and running straight to the other window. He took a deep breath before he took a flying leap straight out of it.

"JOE!" Pat screamed just as Bardy got a good hold of her and carried her down the steps.

Joe had jumped out of windows before, but never on the third floor—not when there wasn't a pool below or something else to break his fall. He'd read somewhere that you could lessen the impact by rolling in midair. Well, whoever said that was apparently an idiot who'd never jumped out of a window in their life.

He rolled as soon as he felt himself fly the air—a front flip that would make any amateur gymnast proud—but it did nothing to numb the impact of the ground as he hit it. If anything, it made the fall worse, more painful. Joe could hear the sickening sound of the bones in his legs cracking as he reached the ground. His spine tingled as if pins and needles were stuck all along it, and the pain as his head connected with the ground was like nothing he'd ever felt before. He saw stars appear in front of his eyes. The entire world went silent for a long moment and he thought he died.

He closed his eyes, welcoming it. He'd done what he'd come here to accomplish. The result was lying about a foot away, in worse shape than him, no doubt. He attempted to turn his head but everything hurt and even with his eyes closed he felt his world spinning on its access. So he just lay there, waiting for death to claim him.

As he waited, a ringing started in his ears, muffled crying rising over it. He started to slowly come back to the world, his eyes creaking open, the world blurried until he blinked a couple times and then...

"Ann?" Joe croaked. "Ann, what—?"

"No," Ann whimpered, placing a finger over his lips. "Don't speak, Joe. You're going to be alright, okay? There's an ambulance on the way; they said not to move you." Joe tried to not but that caused even more pain so he settled for breathing. Ann sniffled. "Oh Joe," she sighed. "Joe, you can't leave me. Not now. I need you, baby. You need to hold out; just a little longer."

"Can't," Joe croaked. "Dying."

"No!" Ann cried. "No, you're not; don't say that."

"But, I-I am," he replied. "And th-that's okay."

"No, it's not!" Ann sobbed. "Don't say that! Please don't say that!" Joe shut his eyes and took a breath. When he opened them again, Pat was there. He turned to look at her.

"Pat," he sighed. "Take...take care of her for me, will ya?"

"Don't talk like that, Joey," Pat sniffled. "You're gonna be just fine, alright? Just fine."

"No," Joe sighed. "I'm not. And if...when I'm not here to protect her...you've gotta...okay? Promise me."

"Joe, I—"

"*Promise*," Joe growled.

Pat took a shuddering breath. "Okay," she said. "I promise."

"Good," Joe breathed, turning his eyes back to Ann.

"She'll take good care of you, okay?" he said. Ann nodded, tearfully.

"So will you," she insisted. "You promised. You promised everything would be alright."

Joe sighed. "I'm sorry," he said. "I don't think I'm...I'm going to be able to..." he trailed off and took another breath. "I'm sorry," he said, closing his eyes. After a long, tense moment, they opened again. "Ann," he breathed. "I...I have to tell you something."

"What?" Ann asked, leaning down again. His voice was becoming faint.

"I...I loved you," Joe breathed out, before his eyes shut permanently and his body went completely limp.

Both Pat and Ann dissolved into tears, the former holding the latter as Ann held on to Joe's body, their tears mingling as they fell to his chest. Above their wails, ambulance sirens could be heard.

THE END

TWO KILLERS & A HOOKER

112

JAKE MICHAELS

CHAPTER ONE

Jesse James Hewitt never knew when the killings would come.

All he knew was that violence was the only tool he had.

He wasn't like other serial killers who stalked their victims and preplanned their attacks. Jesse's victims were random, in all shapes, sizes and colors.

That is how he stayed under the radar.

But his hair trigger temper could go off at any time. Right now, as he parked the stolen Toyota Camry in front of the corner grocery store, he felt happy. He had a little money in his pocket and for the next week had a place to stay at his uncle's pad.

Jesse James did, in fact, look like a modern Jesse James. He wore flared out jeans with a leather vest over a blue denim shirt. He ditched the skin head look years ago and instead grew his hair out long, a tousled mop of brown curls that he rarely combed. He had ice blue eyes that charmed many a woman until they got to know the man behind the eyes and soon felt repulsed.

Jesse walked into the store and noticed the young Asian kid leafing through the latest X-men in front of the comic rack.

He approached the young man, startling him as he craned his neck to look at his comic book cover.

"Wolverine and Kitty Pryde!" Jesse said. "Yeah, I'd fuck her."

Walking through the store, Jesse whistled in tune with the Taylor Swift swing that played on the overhead radio. Bored, he picked up a loaf of Wonderbread off the shelf then tossed it aside. Heading toward the beverage aisle, he reached inside the glass and picked up a bottle of his favorite drink.

Chocolate Yoo-Hoo.

He ripped off the lid and guzzled the contents down, the chocolate milk dripping off the side of his mouth.

Belching loud, he drifted over to the second of the three store aisles, grabbing a box of chocolate donuts. His thick fingers ripped through the plastic, breaking off a piece of a donut.

Jesse looked out at the store front window as a police car sped down the street, sirens blaring. Another squad car followed, then another.

"Uh oh," Jesse cried out. "The natives are restless."

Jesse tossed a chunk of the chocolate donut into his mouth before placing the box on the cashier's counter. An Ethiopian girl, no more than twenty years old, gave him a courtesy smile which quickly disappeared. She had caramel-colored skin and had dyed her hair blonde, leaving the tips dark brown. Her name tag read 'Naomi'.

"Hi," Jesse said.

"You find everything okay?" she asked.

"Definitely," he said, eyeballing the slim young woman up and down. "Anybody ever tell you that you look like Jessica Alba?"

"Who?"

"You know, the actress. Full lips. Beautiful face. If she were black, you'd look just like her. Or maybe she'd look just like you."

"I don't know who you're talking about," Naomi said.

"That's charming," he said. "Where are you from?"

"Ethiopia."

"I would have guessed Eritrea," he said, guzzling down the Yoo-Hoo.

"I need to scan it," she said, holding her hand out.

"Oh right," he said, handing the bottle to the young woman.

"Do you like your job?"

"Will this be all, sir?" Naomi asked, ignoring his question.

"No," Jesse said. "You're a beautiful girl and I'm really interested in how you got here and where you're going. What time do you get off?"

"When do I get off?"

"As often as you can, right?" Jesse laughed loud.

Naomi rolled her eyes.

He looked back at the storefront window. "Open twenty-four seven. How about you? Are you open twenty-four seven?"

"Is this your best game?"

"You couldn't handle my game with a referee and a whistle."

Naomi punched buttons on the cash register. "That will be five dollars."

"Think about it," he said. "You. Me. A glass of scotch in front of a warm fire."

"I don't think so."

"Can you look me in the eye when you say that?"

Naomi complied with his request, her facial expression annoyed. "I'll say this real slow so that you can understand. I. Don't. Think. So."

"I have to take you out," Jesse said. "Sometimes, you meet a person and you just know, do you know what I mean, baby?"

"Five dollars, asshole."

"Asshole," Jesse said, his eyes flickering from lust to hatred. "Is that what I am?"

"Sometimes you meet a person and you just know, do you know what I mean?"

"I just hate it," Jesse said, pulling out his gun. "When people come to this country."

He fired into the girl's stomach.

"And they don't see that I'm a local boy that made good."

Jesse grabbed his box of donuts and headed out of the store, leaving Naomi writhing in pain on the floor. The Asian boy dropped the comic and cowered in fear.

Jesse sneered at the young man then feinted as if he were about to shoot him.

"Boo!"

The Asian kid bolted out of the store, running across the street and into traffic. Horns blared.

"Run!" Jesse laughed, blowing the coils of smoke away from his gun. "Run, China Boy, Run!"

CHAPTER TWO

Kelly had walked up and down the liquor aisle for over a half-hour now. Usually, there would be someone in his face asking if he needed help. But this storekeeper seemed content to watch the television up on the corner wall. An obese woman with tinted eyeglasses she stared up at the television screen oblivious to her surroundings.

Kelly knew the feeling. He felt like everything around him was television and that he was an uncredited player in the script. His emotions felt as if they were trapped in quicksand, his tumultuous childhood traumatizing his brain into an endless loop of bad memories.

A permanent nightmare.

Kelly thought he looked inconspicuous. He wore a Golden State Warriors baseball cap and a long black trench coat two sizes too big. Wire-rimmed glasses covered his face which he always kept downcast, giving him the look of a schoolyard pervert. Underweight and undersized, Kelly cultivated the creepy look. It kept people away from him.

"I can't do it," he muttered. "I can't fucking do it."

He went up and down the aisle again but this time he grabbed the bottle of 'two buck Chuck' and hid it inside his trench coat.

"You can do it," he hissed. "Just fucking do it."

He turned down the aisle again.

"No, I can't," Kelly placed the bottle back on the shelf.

"What the fuck are you doing?" Jesse asked, blocking the path of the young man.

"Excuse me?"

"You don't want the booze?"

"No, sir."

"What's wrong with it."

"I'm trying to give it up."

"Everybody's trying to give something up," Jesse said, taking the bottle of Two Buck Chuck back off the shelf. "That's why everybody is so damn miserable. You gotta do the things you love!"

Kelly looked over at the cashier who sat oblivious to their conversation. He saw that her name tag read 'Rosie'.

"See this?" Jesse asked, holding up the bottle of Chocolate Yoo-hoo. "My dentist says I have to stop drinking these. Causes a bunch of cavities. And heart disease. But I can't stop myself. Tastes too damn good. Want to try?"

Kelly shook his head.

Jesse took another swig of his chocolate then eyeballed the wine bottle. "2014. Vintage! You like the old stuff?"

"Yes, sir."

Jesse popped open the cork. "Here," he said, extending the bottle to Kelly. "Try it."

Kelly looked away, a nervous tic in his neck.

"What's wrong? Cat got your tongue?"

"No, sir."

"You got issues," Jesse said, watching Kelly twitch as he started to back down the aisle.

"What's wrong now?" Jesse asked.

Kelly backed into a Mexican woman with a cart full of six packs. She looked to be nine months pregnant.

"Damn, *mamacita*," Jesse said as the woman walked by. "Way to start the kid off right."

"*Chinga tu madre*," the woman said.

"*Adios, amiga*," Jesse rolled his eyes, walking toward Kelly. "You see, that is what I'm talking about. Poor kid has a mother that is boozing it up and he isn't even out of the womb yet. He's got no chance, that kid. Starting off life behind the eight-ball with a mother like that, right?"

Kelly nodded his head in agreement.

"Come on," Jesse said, motioning Kelly to follow him. "You're a cool dude. Good listener. Sometimes you look at somebody and you just know, you know what I mean?"

The two stepped over to the cashier who never took her eye off the television. A game of Jeopardy was on.

Jesse handed the woman a $20 bill for the $15 bottle.

"Here you are, ma'am," he said. "Keep the change."

The cashier rolled her eyes.

"I think you and I are on the same frequency," Jesse said, leading Kelly out of the store. "Are you from the Bay Area?"

"No sir," Kelly said.

"Well, we don't have that in common. But that's okay."

He handed the bottle of wine to Kelly. "Are there houses of ill-repute where you're from?"

"What's that?"

"No worries, buddy, no worries," Jesse said. "I'm going to show you the time of your damn life. Gonna be like two sailors out on leave. That's right. That's just what we're going to do."

The cashier turned her head away from the television as a news report came on.

The reporter talked about a serial killer on the loose. White male, black baseball cap and glasses.

Rosie paid no mind to the broadcast, she walked to the front door and flipped over the closed sign.

The West Oakland sky had darkened, leaving blood orange hues of pollution on the horizon.

"Look at this shit," Jesse said as they walked down the street outside the liquor store. He shook his head as he gazed upon the abandoned storefronts and houses covered in graffiti. "Street art, my ass. Bunch of crap. Broken windows. Broken condoms. Broken lives. The fuck is wrong with these people?"

Kelly looked unnerved as the light in front of them turned red.

"Come on," Jesse said, crossing against the light. "What are you a Boy Scout?"

Kelly squinted as he looked up at the red light.

"Let's go, dude."

The light turned green and he continued to follow Jesse, not knowing why.

"Where you parked?" Jesse asked.

"I don't have a car."

"You walked? This is a dangerous place for a white boy. I mean we can walk down the streets here in Oakland and nothing will happen to us. Maybe. But absence of evidence isn't evidence of absence. We walk around here long enough someone will try and rob us. That's why we have to stick together. Can't be walking around alone, just one white boy against ten of them-"

"I take the bus," Kelly said. "I have a disability."

"Disability? What kind?"

"Mental."

"Like, you see psychiatrists and shit?"

"Yes, sir."

"Are you crazy?"

"No, sir. I just see and dream about things. And I do things. Sometimes I can't remember if it was real or a dream."

"But you do see a psychiatrist?"

"Yes, sir."

"They worth the money?"

"County pays for it. Plus I get a free bus pass."

"Right on," Jesse said. "Hey, if everyone else in this city gets freebies so can we. People around here are so ugly they make my eyes hurt. They can give them all the welfare they want as long as I don't have to see them. Man, if I were president I would change things, that's for shit-sure. I would test out bio-weapons here. You know, chemicals and shit. Release it into the atmosphere, turn these assholes into mutants. Kinda like the Island of Dr. Moreau. It would be awesome."

"Yes, sir."

"Well, will you look at that."

The two stop in front of a parked Mercedes. Jesse pointed at the bumper sticker that read "Co-Exist" and "Peace."

"See that's what I'm talking about," Jesse said. "Can you believe this shit? Perfectly good German car and they put all that shit on there. Co-exist? Muslims are taking over our damn country and we got assholes with bumper stickers promoting-"

Working himself into a fury, Jesse kicked in the rear brake light before finishing his sentence.

The car alarm went off and startled Kelly.

"Teee haaaawww!" Jesse said, smashing in the other brake light. "Come on!"

Kelly followed Jesse as they ran over to a dilapidated Toyota Camry across the street. The license plate read BAD AZZ.

"This is me," Jesse said, walking to the passenger side door and unlocking it. "Saw the license plate and just had to have it."

"I can't go with you, sir."

"Why not? I think you're cool."

"I don't know you, sir."

"I ain't a fag. Do you think I'm a fag?"

"No, sir."

"Well, let's do this," Jesse reached into his back holster and took out his gun, taking the clip out and then shoving it back in. "Now get in the fuckin' car and let's get rowdy like good sailors should."

Kelly nodded and got into the vehicle.

"Nice to see you changed your mind," Jesse said, hiding the gun in his back pocket again. "Only fools and the dead never changed their mind."

CHAPTER THREE

Jesse drove down the street like a maniac, alternately speeding up then slowing down. He swerved in front of cars, flipping the bird indiscriminately.

Kelly stared straight ahead looking scared shitless.

"Look man, I didn't mean to pull the gun on you," Jesse said. "I promised you a good time, right? We gonna get some whores. Show you what a cool guy I am. How's that sound?"

Kelly shrugged his shoulders.

"The Warriors ain't playing tonight," Jesse pointed at Kelly's baseball cap. "You watch the game last night?"

"No."

"Me neither," Jesse said. "Shit, why do that when you can go out and get some poontang, you know what I mean?"

Jesse looked out the side window and saw a blonde woman walking down the street. Dressed in business attire, her suit did little to conceal her figure.

"Holy shit!" Jesse slowed the vehicle down. "Curves for days!"

The woman turned her head and looked at the men staring at her.

"Hey darlin'" Jesse said.

Rolling her eyes, the woman turned around and began walking in the opposite direction.

"Well, fuck you then," Jesse laughed. "We could have you cumming instead of going, ain't that right, friend?"

Looking up ahead, Jesse saw a brunette walking, her eyes focused on her cell phone.

"Hot, hot, hot," Jesse said. "All these young Cal students out here sometimes. Usually trying to score some dope. What is your type? Me? I don't really have a type. I like them all really. Tall, short. Big ass. Little ass. I just like pulling girls hair. That's what gets me off. It's primal, you know. Doggy style."

They slow down and see a prostitute up ahead. She's blonde, very tall and leaning up against the pole of a bus stop.

Upon seeing Jesse's car slowing down, she twirled around the pole, like a stripper.

"Here we go," Jesse lowered his voice. "Think we might have a live one here."

Jesse stopped the vehicle next to the woman who poked her head in on the passenger side.

"Hey boys, you need a date?"

Her face had pock-marks, as if she had small-pox. Her half-lidded jaundice eyes a dead giveaway of her crack whore status.

Jesse slammed on the gas. "Good God! Did you see that? I've seen ugly but goddamn! And she had no teeth! Then again she doesn't need teeth for what she does!"

Jesse looked over at Kelly and noticed him staring at a different brunette up ahead. The girl stood with her arms crossed, emphasizing her ample cleavage.

"There you go," Jesse said. "There you go."

He stopped the car in front of the woman.

Upon closer inspection, her hair was dark blonde with brown streaks. A light skinned Latina, with full lips and green eyes. In her mid-twenties, she smiled wide as Jesse drove up.

"Two good looking guys in here. How's it going?"

"Will you do the things she won't?" Jesse asked.

"I'm the girl your mami and your papi warned you about," she said. Her voice breathy, with an accented lilt, like a breeze combing through dry leaves on a hot summer night.

"What's good on the menu?"

"That depends on how hungry you boys are," the woman said, reaching down and grabbing Kelly's crotch on 'hungry.'

Kelly shuddered in fear.

"My friend over here is starving," Jesse laughed. "As in he has not had a meal in years, if you catch my drift."

"Well, there will be plenty on the plate for both of you."

"Hop in, *mamacita*," Jesse said.

Kelly watched as the woman got into the car. His heart began to pound and his throat began to feel parched, her sweet perfume quickly filling the vehicle.

Reminding him of his mother.

CHAPTER FOUR

"My name is Maricela," she said from the backseat, looking over at Kelly on the passenger side.

Kelly said nothing, holding the wine bottle to his chest and pursing his lips.

"Is he mute?" Maricela asked Jesse. "Or deaf?"

"He doesn't open up until he really trusts someone," Jesse said. "He's smart that way. Do you always judge people?"

"I'm not judging," Maricela said. "Just asked him a damn question."

"Now you're trying to make him feel bad," Jesse said. "You're supposed to make us feel good. Make me and him feel like kings. Right, Kelly?"

Jesse reached over and playfully hit Kelly in the arm.

"I'll do that and more," Maricela said.

"Damn skippy," Jesse said. "Tee haaawww!"

"You're not high are you?" she asked.

"I'm high on life," Jesse said. "Hangin' with my homie here and about to bust a nut on a fine ass Latina."

"Well, thank you, handsome."

"Here," Jesse reached over and took the wine bottle out of Kelly's hand. "Let's get this party started."

Kelly grabbed the wine back, agitated.

"I didn't mean what I said," Maricela said to Kelly, running her fingers through the hair underneath his cap. "You seem nice. And cute. Sometimes you just know, you know what I mean? You look at someone and you get a feeling about them. It is a survival trait among us escorts."

Kelly pulled back then gave in to the woman's touch.

"There you go," Jesse said. "My friend here is an introvert. Just takes some time before he opens up to you."

"I've seen it all, dude, believe me," Maricela said. "There was this guy the other night who wanted me to shave off his chest hair. And there was this other dude that wanted me to take out this dildo he had shoved up his ass. When I took it out, the dildo was still vibrating."

"Sick fucker," Jesse said. "What a sick fuck."

"Can you imagine shoving a dildo up your ass and than calling an escort to fish it out?" Maricela asked.

"My imagination can't go that far," Jesse said.

"Maybe he called one escort to put it in and then called another to take it out?" Kelly asked.

"There you go," Jesse said. "See? He needs to get to know you before he talks."

"There's my place," Kelly said, pointing in the distance.

The television was already on when the trio stepped inside. A news reporter held up a bottle of Charles Shaw wine, explaining how forensics determined the amount of poison that a serial killer used to murder his victims.

"Nice!" Jesse said as he entered Kelly's house. Faded flowered prints marked the wallpaper but Kelly had no pictures or paintings, only one mirror in the center of the living room.

Maricela walked over to the mirror, dabbing her make-up and adjusting her cleavage.

"This is a nice place, friend," Jesse said. "I can spend lots of time up in here. We can watch TV, play video games, shoot the shit. Do you have an X-Box? My kind of place here."

Kelly said nothing as he entered the kitchen and set the wine bottle down, half-listening as Jesse continued to jabber on.

On the counter, he saw the rat poison and weed killer boxes next to the wine bottle. He quickly grasped the incriminating evidence and shoved them into his trench coat.

"Not a bad view," Jesse said, opening than closing the window curtain. "This place is what blue collar is supposed to look like. Nothing fancy. Just warm coziness. This is America! Shit man, we should go out and get an apple pie to go with that wine."

"You sound like a politician," Maricela said.

"I am the King," Jesse said. "A king. Have you ever been to L.A.?

"Yeah, I go down south sometimes."

"I was there last month. Hollywood. What a bunch of freaks! I went there thinking I could get away from all these Occupy Idiots and what happens? I get caught up in their protest! Wanted to shoot every one of those tree-hugging bitches!"

Kelly placed the poison inside a cabinet and tried to step back out of the kitchen when Jesse stepped in front of him.

"Freakin' idiots!" Jesse screamed in Kelly's face. "Do you know what I mean? These fuckers should go out and get a damn job. Am I right?"

"Right," Kelly nodded his head.

"That's right, buddy," Jesse said, sidestepping Kelly and entering the kitchen. "What kind of grub you got, man?"

Jesse ignored the ant trail on the counter and opened the refrigerator. "What kind of goodies do we have going on in here?"

Kelly crossed and uncrossed his arms, looking nervous.

"Nice!" Jesse said. "Hey man, there is only one ice cream flavor in the world. Only one. Care to guess?"

Kelly shook his head.

Jesse took out an ice cream carton from the freezer in triumph. "Vanilla! Damn, we have a lot in common."

Jesse opened up one of the drawers and grabbed a spoon.

"Come on," Jesse said. "Let's get the party started."

The two walked back into the living room.

Maricela has her shirt off, standing there wearing nothing but a black bra and jeans.

"Wow," Jesse said.

"You like?"

"Nice artwork," Jesse's eyes scanned up and down Maricela's tattooed body. A snake went down her left arm and she had pentagrams on both shoulders. "You're a devil woman."

"I got into the occult in college," Maricela said, looking down at her own tattoos. "Did a mid-term paper on this occult in Mexico then I got interested in the stuff. This one here is the eye of horus."

Maricela pointed down at her belly-button, the Egyptian symbol of protection inked on her stomach.

"So gentleman," she said. "Are we going one at a time or is this a threesome?"

"My friend here goes first," Jesse said, scooping out a spoonful of the ice cream and letting holding it out to Maricela. "Let's make it special."

Maricela wrapped her lips around the spoon, sucking off the ice cream as she sat down on the chair behind her.

"No," Kelly squealed.

Maricela sprang out of the seat.

"Not that chair!" he yelled.

Maricela stepped away from the chair and gave Jesse a startled look. "Are you sure he's alright?"

"I said don't judge him," Jesse said before taking a few steps back with the young man. "You hearing voices?"

"Loud and clear," Kelly said.

"Alright now," Jesse said. "That's nothing to be ashamed of. You should be proud of that. Been hearing voices all your life and you're still here. You're a damn soldier."

"I am?"

"Hell fucking yeah," Jesse said. "But she'll help you get rid of those voices, okay?"

Jesse patted Kelly on the back before heading into the kitchen.

"Relax, dude," Maricela whispered.

Kelly slowly turned his back to the young woman but she spun him around gently.

"It is really easy," Maricela said, taking Kelly by the hand. "First timers are my specialty."

She lead him to the chair to sit down and he shuddered.

"Easy," Maricela said. "We don't have to do it there."

She placed her hands on both of his shoulders and led him over to the couch.

Kelly sat down, eyes downcast.

Maricela played with unbuckling his belt until he turned away.

"Okay, okay, we can do other things."

She let the strap of her bra fall down off her shoulder.

Kelly looked up with painful shyness, licking his cracked lips as he stared at Maricela's breasts.

"You're a titty man," she laughed. "There you go."

Maricela took his hand and placed it on her left breast, letting the young man knead away.

"Gently," she said, tilting her head back in pleasure. "Gently. There you go. You like that?"

Kelly nodded, noticing the upside down cross that Maricela had tattooed on the underside of her wrist.

"Me too, baby. Me too."

Kelly turned to the kitchen door and shuddered as he saw Jesse standing there, watching.

"What are you doing?" Jesse asked. "I said he is a beginner. He's shy with women. You gotta take it slow."

"You get off on taking a front row seat?" Maricela asked. "We were taking it slow."

"Then why is he so freaked out?"

Maricela glared at Jesse.

"Come on," Jesse said, waving her away from the couch. "Give us a minute here. Go upstairs to the bedroom and we'll be right there. We need to have a man to man."

Maricela got up off the couch, rolling her eyes as she made her way up the steps.

"This always works for me," Jesse said, waving the wine bottle in his hand as he sat down next to Kelly. "Loosens you up. Breaks down whatever blockages you got going on in your big head and little head."

Kelly gulped hard.

"We'll be right there!" Jesse called out. "Go ahead and get nekkid! He'll be right up."

CHAPTER FIVE

Maricela entered the bedroom and closed the door. The lamp on the desk illuminated the neatly made bed. There were pictures of dead bugs on the wall which gave her the creeps. She looked closer and realized that they weren't pictures at all. They were dead moths and butterflies inserted between the glass and cardboard backing.

A buck is a buck, she thought, seeing more than her share of strange. She walked over to the TV set and pushed the button to turn it on, looking for the remote control on the counter.

"Look man," Jesse said, putting his arm around Kelly like a big brother. "There is only one thing you need to know about women, okay? You have to satisfy their needs. Once you do that, you are in. Okay? So do you know what women want more than anything?"

"Help?"

"No, they want to get high," Jesse said, removing his arm around Kelly, struggling to uncork the wine bottle he held between his legs. "You just have to find out what women want. Some women you meet are going to want fun. Power. Status. Money. That is why whores like

Maricela are so great. There is no drama. You pay your fee and get what you want."

Jesse popped the cork on the bottle and Kelly shuddered. He knew he had placed the poison in that one.

Jesse raised the bottle to his lips but Kelly grabbed it out of his hands.

"No!"

Jesse stared at Kelly for a beat.

"You never got to have any fun did you?" Jesse asked.

"She used to send me to the store," Kelly said. "With a note to get booze."

"Your mom?"

Kelly nodded.

"No worries, man," Jesse said, moving closer to Kelly now. "My folks were the same way. Both of them alcoholics. Dad was a functional one. Went to work every day. Worked his ass off every day. Then one day he shot himself. Just stepped into the house and blew his brains out. Died all alone."

"I never knew my Dad. Never. No pictures. Nothing. Bet he died alone."

"My mom didn't even cry," Jesse said. "Just kept bringing men over. Fucked every one. Didn't care if I was listening or watching or what. Definitely didn't care that my Dad found out. She was evil, man. Evil incarnate."

"Mine too," Kelly whispered, hunching his back as of the ghost of his mother could hear him.

"Mine was worse than an evil step mom. She was a real mom."

Maricela laid on the bed, noodling around on her cell phone which now showed a dead battery. Looking around for an extension so she could recharge it, the screen shot on the television caught her eye.

The report showed a police sketch of a man that resembled Jesse.

"Police said to be on the lookout for the license plate BAD AZZ in a late model white or gray Toyota. If you have any information regarding the suspect please call 911 immediately."

Maricela toggled on her cell phone again. Dead.

She ran over to the bedroom door but when he opened it she saw Jesse standing outside with Kelly behind him.

"Someone is in a hurry to get started," Jesse said. "If you're that horny you can go ahead and start without us."

"Was just wondering where you guys were," she said.

"He's ready and rarin' to go," Jesse said, placing his arm around Kelly and shaking him. "Go get 'em, Tiger."

Maricela forced a smile, stepping aside to let the men in.

"You ready to show him a good time?" Jesse asked.

"But of course," she said, her voice quavered, betraying her nervousness. "Give the man a little privacy."

Maricela took Kelly by the hand and led him further into the bedroom. She attempted to close the door but Jesse stopped her.

"Nothing goes on behind closed doors around here," Jesse said.

Kelly looked back at Jesse as if he were about to go into the electric chair.

"You can do it, buddy!"

"Come on, handsome," Maricela motioned for Kelly to sit down on the bed. The young man took a deep breath, eyes downcast until he slowly looked up at woman stroking his upper thigh. "Do you think I'm pretty?" she asked.

Kelly could only nod his head, smitten by her beauty.

"Thanks," she said.

Jesse made as if he were going down the steps but stopped at the top, kneeling down so he remained out of Maricela's eyeline.

He listened to Maricela's voice, his heart beating in anticipation of what came next just like when his mother had men over at the house.

"You look like a movie star," Kelly blurted out. "Like you should be in porn or something."

"We should go someplace else," Maricela said. "Just the two of us. Okay?"

"But what about my friend? You don't like him?"

"I like you better," she said, kissing him on the lips then hugging him.

Kelly shuddered in delight.

"You have to leave," she said, nuzzling his ear. "This dude is a serial killer. Okay? He'll kill us both."

"What the hell is going on here?" Jesse asked stepping through the door, his entire body an antennae telling him that something was up.

"This young stud is pitching up a tent!" Maricela said, standing back up and pointing at Kelly's crotch.

Jesse grabbed her wrist before she could walk back downstairs. "Where are you going?"

"I have to get us some protection. Duh." Maricela hurried out of the bedroom.

Jesse sat down next to Kelly. "What did she say to you?"

"She has a crush on me."

"Ha!" Jesse laughed. "See? See what happens when you give women what they want. You gonna start listening to me now?"

They both hear Maricela's high heels running down the steps.

Jesse sprinted down the stairs and caught her just as she reached the door.

He spun her around, angry. "It ain't polite to leave a party early! Thought you were going to get some protection?"

"I left the rubbers in the car."

"Left the rubbers in the car, bullshit!" Jesse slammed her against the wall. "You're a damn devil. A thief!"

Jesse reached inside Maricela's purse and pulled out a wallet.

Kelly's wallet.

"Stop!" Kelly said, coming down the steps.

"Lifted it straight outta your pocket, dude!" Jesse threw the wallet back at Kelly.

Maricella ran over to the wine bottle on the coffee table and smashed it against the edge. Grasping the bottle by the handle, she held it in front of her as a weapon.

"Ooooh," Jesse said. "Come on, bitch! Come on, let's see what you got!"

Maricela's face contorted into that of feral woman, fighting for her life. She stabbed at Jesse, lacerating his hand with the glass.

"Bitch!" he said.

Maricela ran toward the kitchen.

Jesse gave chase until Kelly jumped on his back.

"Leave her alone!" Kelly screamed.

Jesse threw off the little man with ease, pushing him into the chair. "You crazy? This bitch just tried to rob you, man!"

Racing through the kitchen, Maricela opened the cellar door and locked it behind herself.

"Bitch!" Jesse screamed, pounding on the wood. "Bitch!"

He kicked the cellar door again and again.

"Fuck off!" Maricela cried out.

Jesse looked down at his hand, his blood dripping on the kitchen floor.

Walking back into the living room, he saw Kelly sitting on the couch watching TV, another wine bottle in his hand.

"Dude!" Jesse said, holding up his bloodied hand. "Look what your damn girlfriend did to me."

"She's not my girlfriend."

"Where's the key to your basement?" Jesse asked, taking out his gun. "Or do I have to just blow shit open?"

"I have the key," Kelly said, glaring at Jesse.

"Hey man," Jesse said. "You're looking at me with some hate in your eye. I told you that girl was a thief. A demon. You see that upside cross on her wrist? She's a devil worshiper! Doesn't Satanism freak you the fuck out? Let's go kill her ass."

"She's already dead," Kelly said, staring off into the distance, in his own world.

"All of mine are dead too," Jesse said pointing the gun at his own temple. "So let's kill another one."

"She told me she loved me."

"Of course," Jesse said. "I knew that. That's why I got her for you. Figured she was just your type."

He took the wine bottle out of Kelly's hand and guzzled it down. "Aaaaahhh!"

Kelly returned his attention to the television, his eyes transfixed.

"What is it, goddamnit?" Jesse asked, turning toward the TV. He saw the police sketch of himself and the license plate.

BAD AZZ.

Enraged, he shot a bullet through the TV.

CHAPTER SIX

Maricela heard the gunshot. Startled, she looked around the cellar for a weapon of any kind. She found a fire poker in the corner and gripped it hard.

Kelly ran back toward the cellar door with the keys in hand. "I'll get you out," he called out to Maricela. "I'll help you."

Jesse chased after him but fell down, the room spinning, his entire body sweating. He retched again, with blood streaked bile coming out of his mouth. He looked at Kelly staring at him, wild-eyed with fear. His friend went in and out of focus, doubling and distorting like a kaleidoscope.

What was in that wine?

Maricela took the fire poker and smashed out the tiny cellar windows.

"Help me!" she screamed. "I've been kidnapped! Help me!"

Kelly put the key in the cellar lock but could not get it to open.

Jesse pitched forward over the sink and retched again.

"The fuck you put into that wine?" Jesse asked, purple bile spilling out of his mouth.

"I'm sorry," Kelly said.

Falling to the ground, Jesse pointed the gun at Kelly.

"I was just trying to be a good friend," Jesse said.

Maricela screamed as she heard the gunshot.

She scrambled back up the cellar steps. Pressing her ear to the door, she waited several minutes before she unlocked it.

Opening up the door, she saw both Jesse and Kelly on the floor in a growing pool of blood.

Kelly laid on his stomach, the blood spewing forth from the fatal gunshot blast into his belly. He stared straight ahead at Jesse who laid on his back, blood and foam caked around his lips, neck and chest.

Ants began to scuttle over their bodies.

They were both locked in a death stare at each other. The pupils of their eyes like black holes eating the whites.

Their once lonely faces no longer dark but relieved.

They didn't have to die alone.

KISS THE SUN

JESSICA OLSEN

The heist had been planned for months, almost a year. Julian was the ringleader, but all of them had been thinking of it for while.

Rock lost his job during the last series of factory shutdowns. His parents had been of the mentality that there would always been work in manual labor and had never been particularly bothered by his poor grades. He had trusted them and his trust had backfired. As the years went by, work in his field of expertise dried up. He retrained again and again, moving from factory to factory as he was repeatedly replaced by machines. His work was reduced to minimum wage jobs in warehouses. He had considered moving to the country and working on a farm, but jobs there were drying up too. He was terrified of leaving the home he knew and the people he liked to spend the rest of his life picking strawberries on a by the pound salary. When Julian had suggested the heist, Rock was in. He had considered turning to crime before, but had never known anyone to cooperate with and didn't really feel he had the intellect to pull it off. Julian on the other hand, overshadowed Rock in intelligence, background knowledge and the contacts they needed. Rock trusted Julian implicitly. And at that stage, he didn't really have a choice any more.

Electra had been roped into it less willingly than Rock could have suspected. She and Julian had been together for two years when he came up with the plan, but she felt it may be time to move on. Julian was intelligent, talented and educated. He was also amazingly good looking. She had been drawn in by his gorgeous dark locks and green eyes and she had stayed in hopes that his talent would eventually lead to a big-time breakthrough. After the first year, her hopes had begun to fade. She had found Julian to be lazy and arrogant. She had also found him to be very good at spending all his money on alcohol and strip clubs. Over the second year she had drifted away. Coming to terms with her plumpening figure and the first grays on her head, she had started looking elsewhere, wondering what her life would have been like if she'd chosen better. When Julian had first proposed the plan she had laughed in his face, packed a small bag and spent the night at her best friend's house. But he patiently waited until she had thought it through and, as she considered it, the prospect of her cut, a cool four hundred thousand, was inviting. She wasn't sure whether she'd stay with him afterward, but she was happy to string along for another few months if there was a chance she could get all that. It was better than going back to selling weed anyway.

Harry Julian was the mastermind. As Electra had found out, despite his intellect, talent and several hundred thousand dollars worth of business school, he wasn't particularly interested in hard graft. He came up with numerous plans and get rich quick schemes. He bought and sold flats, invested in shares, started a nation wide weed business and turned his hand to running a bailiff company. Many of them were successful. But after they succeeded he would drain the funds and go on holiday where he would get drunk and visit strip clubs until the money was all gone and he was back at step one. When nothing was left he wanted to do something new. Only this time he felt he had an edge. He had spent many years of internship working at a bank that was currently being remodeled. They had decided to stay open during the refurbishment, leaving several key spots vulnerable. The amount of money the bank held would be less, but still enough for almost one and a half million to be almost within Julian's grasp. This would be the pot of gold he would retire on. Of course, he had to find trustworthy people to help him. He approached a few old business associates, but only one of them, Rock, a mild-mannered, high school dropout of a thug, was happy to go through with it. He wasn't bright enough to help with the planning, but he wasn't bright enough to trick Julian or hand him in either. He would be some use as a getaway driver. Running out of options and always a man of resource, Julian had turned to the one person who, in some body or another, had always helped him: his woman. If things had cooled down and Electra had decided to leave Julian would have waited to build rapport with another girl and probably got bored of the idea before he had enough people to go through with the heist. The night she left he had reloaded his dating profile and called a couple of his other dealers. He usually just went out with his old dealer girls due to the rapport they had already built with him, but he was open to new possibilities. There was nothing some women wouldn't do for an intelligent bad boy, as Julian had found since middle school.

The heist was a perfect plan. Electra would distract the cashier during the quiet time of day, when everyone else was upstairs having lunch or outside smoking. Julian insisted she should go as far as she had to in order to keep him distracted. She was hesitant, but somehow he persuaded her. Then again, money was persuasive. She flirted with the cashier for an hour until everyone else had left and he was the only member of staff there. Meanwhile, Julian used the scaffolding to slip past the cameras. The vault was locked, but, as he suspected, the combination method hadn't changed. They just moved the digits around on a monthly basis. Julian went through his old notes and over a few drinks and joints he worked out what the current combination must be. And he was right. He filled two sports bags with as much money as they could hold. Feeling an impulse of greed he also filled his parka and tightened it around the neck and waist.

Somehow he managed to evade the cameras and the staff in his suspicious getup. He made his way to Rocky's car and unloaded the money into the boot as inconspicuously as he could manage. Then he waited in the passenger seat for Electra to appear. After waiting half an hour, she emerged with her hair in a mess and a suspicious smile on her face.

Julian was pretty sure he saw her at the cashier as he was leaving, so if she had stayed behind to do anything else, it was on her. He was expecting her to hop into the car as though nothing happened, but instead she just walked up to it.

"Look babe, I'm gonna go and see a movie, OK? I'll see you back at the house and we can discuss business later."

Julian rolled his eyes. "Sure babes. You could have told us."

Electra shrugged. "I just decided now. If it went well I'd go see a movie, if it didn't, well, I wouldn't, would I?"

"Fine, fine, but we already look suspicious as fuck. Go watch the movie. We'll count the... green and then you can get your cut when you're back."

Electra thought it over. She knew Julian would probably take an extra cut, but she really couldn't care less. As long as she had enough for a nice little house somewhere sunny, she was happy. She slung her bag higher up her shoulder, shrugged again as a sort of farewell and made her way to the cinema.

She didn't know she was being followed.

It hadn't been long before the workers had returned from their smoke and noticed the open vault. They called the police immediately. Paul Sanchez wasn't on duty, but as he parked his car he realized the last report to be radioed in was right opposite his house. But Paul had better things to do. He pretended not to notice and walked towards the door before remembering he had forgotten to get milk. As he turned sharply and walked down the street, a beautiful woman caught his eye. Electra wasn't exactly stunning or a great dresser, but she had that foxy redhead appeal that, when an expert eye landed on it, would turn heads. And Paul was an expert on redheads. He looked her up and down and saw her calmly walk towards the cinema. It couldn't hurt.

Feeling a little sheepish and ashamed of his actions, he quickly crossed the road and, after seeing what room Electra walked into, he bought a ticket. He always used to think of it as odd when young women watched action films but he was finding that, as of late, it was far more common. He sat one row behind her and stared at her hair through the commercials. A deeper investigation revealed it to be dyed, but that didn't matter any more. She was lovely and he spent the movie wondering how to approach her.

Fortunately for him, he didn't need to. With images of the money floating in her head, Electra could taste freedom already and was getting frisky for a fresh man. And with his dark Latin looks and stylish hair and shirt, Paul Sanchez fit the bill: he was her type. She spied him as she was packing her remaining snacks into her bag and impulsively left her number with him. Wordlessly, she left the cinema feeling warm and excited to the pit of her stomach.

Sanchez couldn't believe his luck. He was too nervous and confused to call her that night and decided to play it cool and put it off a few days. That was, until the next day he was assigned the case and discovered that one of the people they were trying to contact was his buxom redhead. She was suspected as an accomplice in bank robbery and either first or second degree murder of a cashier. He was in two minds as to whether to tell anyone, but he figured his job was more important than a possible fling with a potential criminal. He reported to Detective Carl Kenty with the fortunate information. Apparently she had been seen in the bank and outside the bank talking to their prime suspects: a man with dark hair and a pale complexion and a huge man with a farmer's tan and a tattoo on his left arm. Paul was hoping he'd be asked to contact her, but once all the details came out Kenty, destroyer of parties and champion of chastity, instead set Paul Sanchez, Rick McAllister and Paddy "Irish" Dola on watch at her house should the other two suspects appear. Paul would meet up with her at her home and the other two would watch. After all, they would likely bolt at any chance of police intervention and the woman, if she was an accomplice, would bolt just as much as the men. They needed to find her and watch her until she and her associates tried to do a runner. Then they would just have to follow them and catch the marked notes.

As planned, Paul called Electra's number and arranged a date. It was surprisingly easy, making him question whether it was a scam of another variety. Then again, as he was backed by Rick and Paddy, he felt fairly safe entering her home. All it would take was the press of a button and they'd receive an alert that he was in danger and be able to rush the house.

He needn't have worried. Electra invited him into the flat easily and with clear intentions. Not wanting to break his character, or at least that would be what Kenty heard, Paul followed her upstairs for the sort of lovemaking he had never imagined could exist in real life. He thought to himself what a pity it would be if this woman turned out to be an aggressive bank robber. What a pity if she were to go to prison for five, ten, twenty years. What a waste of natural charm and talent.

After he excused himself, he returned to where the others were and added himself to the night-watch rota. Paddy, ever paranoid, was certain something had to go wrong soon. It was all too smooth, too steady. It made no sense. They would hit a snag eventually and he would be there to tell everyone he told them so. Rick told Paddy to mind his work and leave everyone else alone, at which Paddy retreated to standard grumbling.

Later that evening, when Paul was on duty and feeling certain any woman would avoid the dark cover of the barely lit streets, Electra emerged from the flat. She had a note in one hand and her car keys in the other. Paul was confident that nobody else could be home, so wherever she was going, it was likely the other robbers were as well. If she was part of the robbery, that was. As she turned the corner, he ignited the engine and creeped the car behind hers, keeping close but leaving enough space for doubt. Not that there was much point. The streets were so bare that if she paid any attention to him she would notice he was following her. He just hoped she wouldn't, or she wouldn't think anything of it.

But those streets were pretty familiar to him. And the more she drove, the more familiar they became. She was driving towards the bank and back to the scene of the crime. In his head, Paul formulated all sorts of clever reasons why she would return. They left something? That was their meet up point? Maybe it was true that the criminal always returned.

But Electra was driving that way for an entirely different reason. Paul hadn't noticed it, but she had watched him from a café as he made his way home the other night. She had seen the house where he lived and she had seen the police vehicle outside the door. When after their passionate lovemaking she spied him sneaking into a pretty obvious surveillance vehicle opposite her, she had no doubts. Paul was a copper, a police officer, and on her tail in more ways than she was on his.

She had mulled it over. He may be a police officer, but he was very good looking and very charming. She liked their smalltalk and that they shared tastes in music and films. As an upstanding member of the community with a safe job, he was a promising prospect, unlike a certain person. She was determined to make this work somehow.

So she pulled up by his house, stepped outside the car and leaned against his house door. At that point Paul realized what she had been doing. She wasn't returning to the scene, she was returning to him. And branding him a policeman by doing so.

He wasn't sure whether to park and step out or to avoid her entirely, but as her carefully manicured fingernail beckoned him he knew he had no choice. He parked and made his way over to his own house and the dangerous redhead in front of it.

"I knew it, Paulie." She grinned, impressed with herself. "You're police, aren't ya?"

Paul nodded, wincing slightly at the newly-acquired nickname.

"I bet you're after Julian. I should have known he couldn't make good of something like this..." His raised eyebrow caught her eye before he could mask it. "You don't know?"

"Ma'am, cooperating with the police could save you a lot of jail time."

Electra laughed and nodded. "I know, I know. But if you know nothing, you prove nothing."

"Technically I am on duty, so I can use what you say. It would be my word against yours."

Electra smiled widely. "I guess so." She wasn't sure where to go from there. She desperately wanted to spill her guts to Paul and make passionate love to him in his own bed that very instant. He was the sort of man that inspired the deepest heat in her, like Julian had been until he proved his weak character and slovenly nature. But that heat rarely turned out well. If she walked away from the money now and walked into Paul's arms, he could turn out to be another Julian. Then what of her little house in the sun, of her early retirement surrounded by tan pool boys and elite women for continual intellectual and physical stimulation? She would get neither and wind up a spinster. It might be an old-fashioned concept, but the very thought of remaining poor and single into old age tightened her stomach. There was only one way.

"Say, Paulie." She cooed. "Do you find me attractive?"

"I am on duty." Paul reminded her, his eyes scanning her wildly curved figure. "I don't think I need to remind you."

"You were on duty last time you seduced me too." She smirked. "Why can't I seduce you while you're on duty?"

"I suppose I find you attractive." Paul confessed. "Extremely attractive, in fact."

"And do you find money attractive, Paulie?" She continued.

"Everyone finds money attractive, Electra." He smiled back at her. He knew she was going nowhere good, but he was happy to entertain her in case she made another slip like before. Though, in the rush, he had somehow forgotten the name. Willie? Jailer? Wally? He wasn't sure any more. Her curves were doing their magic on him. He forced his eyes to the wall just behind her.

"Then I have an idea." Electra grinned. "How about you help me get the money and I help you get me and the money?"

"And how would that work?" Paul forced the smile to stay put.

"The mastermind behind this whole operation was Julian. He is currently my partner, though Heaven knows I don't want him to be. The only reason I went along with this was because I figured I'd never get caught, but now I'm getting shit for it and he isn't, which is hardly fair. I propose this: you kill Julian. I can give you the address, make it look like it was in the line of duty of whatever you coppers call it. I collect the money. You claim it was already gone and I had nothing to do with it. We both disappear to Barbados and live out our lives under the sun, fucking like rabbits and drinking away our retirement."

Paul was disgusted. At every single aspect of the situation. He was disgusted that Electra already had a partner and was so readily spreading her legs for new men. He was disgusted that she was staying with Julian for the money. He was disgusted that she wanted to kill her partner. He was disgusted that she wanted him to kill for sex and money. He was disgusted at the whole proposition.

"No thank you." He couldn't even bring himself to pretend he would do it. He just wanted to get home and have a cold shower to wash every last trace of her from his body. He pushed past her and opened the door, making his way upstairs.

Electra had reached to grab his buttocks as he walked past but thought better of it. The man didn't want her. She had already said too much and she wasn't sure what would happen if she did anything else. She watched him longingly before bolting home like a deer startled by a car.

The next morning Rock and Julian were round to talk cash. Despite his greedy arms, Julian had only managed to grab one million and a bit. As Julian and Electra argued over the money and how they would split it, Rock assumed his normal position at Electra's window.

He knew Julian was holding out on Electra: they had broken two million. But he also felt Electra deserved it and besides, he had been paid extra to keep his mouth shout and he wasn't a fool. So he left them squabbling and watched Ann through the window, as he usually did. Ann was Electra's neighbor and a mighty attractive girl at that. Rock had spied her one afternoon as he dropped off a bag of weed for Electra to sell and he'd been fascinated ever since. She kept her windows open during the day and often spent whole afternoons in the garden. She was the girl next door type he'd always liked. He'd never really given himself a chance to dream about these things, but now he knew he would be getting eight hundred thousand he felt happier about these dreams. He would have a strawberry field of his own somewhere nice and isolated. And he'd pay his workers a fair wage and overcharge the hippies that wanted organic strawberries. And on his arm he'd have a nice girl like Ann. Maybe even Ann herself. She was a joy to watch. He couldn't get her off his mind.

Paul, on the other hand, couldn't get Electra off his mind for another reason. He wasn't sure what at all to say to Kenty, so he filled it in on his own. He explained he hadn't seen either of the suspects around her and that she had revealed nothing. He was hoping that she would just disappear from his life. Or at least he was on the surface. Internally, a passion he never recalled experiencing before was boiling over. Electra was his perfect woman, the ideal. She had the figure, the flaming red hair and the sexy, fiery temperament. They even shared taste in music and films. She was his dream girl and the longer he spent trying to forget her, the less he could.

Relationships had never went the way Paul Sanchez wanted them to. Ever since middle school, like Julian, Paul had enjoyed girls' attention for his good looks. But unlike Julian Paul had never had a relationship last. Girls and women were drawn in by his dark locks and smoldering gaze, but almost instantly drew away from him. It was as though there were some part of him, some invisible feature that girls discovered in his bare soul. He tried being standoffish. He tried being nice. He tried committing and cheating. And whatever he did, they just moved away. He had come to give up on a stable relationship at all, drifting from girl to girl, continually longing for one to stay, to validate his efforts, to make him feel loved. But none did. They wanted him, but they didn't love him. And he was starting to believe they couldn't.

At least until he met Electra. He saw how different she was. She desired him deeply. She shared enough with him. She was a voraciously sexual being as well as a fragile, emotional woman. She was everything he had been raised to believe a good partner should be. And maybe that was the missing component? Maybe she was just the right woman for him, the one he would have to be with?

He tried to shake the thought but the more he shook it the more it stuck. He became terrified of losing her. He found himself imagining her long legs around his waist, her hand on his thigh as they watched a film, her lips to his ear, whispering sweet nothings... And he was going to throw all this away because of a job? Because he wanted to be a good policeman? He'd tried being good. He'd tried being nice. And what had it got him? A standard salary, a small house and the single life. On the other hand, being bad, being criminal... that would get him his dream girl, his one and only, as well as more money than he was likely to make his entire life.

Paul had to do something. Or she might get away. Desperate, he took advantage of his day off and went to visit Electra. He was as secretive as he could be and he was glad about it too. Outside the house, still watching intently, was Rick in the police car. Clearly the front door wasn't an option, so, trying to stay hidden from the pretty girl in the garden opposite as well as from Rick's perfect vantage point, Paul slipped between the fences and down towards Electra's shared garden. Once there he tried looking for the red bohemian curtain he remembered from their lovemaking. The thoughts were still fresh in his mind and he quickly identified the window. He messaged her asking her to let him in. The window slid ajar and he clumsily made his way up the fire escape and slipped right in.

Electra was alone again. She wasn't about to tell Paul that Julian and Rock had just left the way he came or that she knew about the car still outside her house. She wasn't going to help him, however daringly romantic this gesture was.

Paul couldn't help himself and before he managed to utter even a whisper of the plan, he had her beneath him in the bed and he was breathing a sigh of relief into the kiss. She was a sweet aphrodisiac, a drug, an ambrosia. He needed her. Pulling his head back, he looked her straight in the eye. "I'll do it."

"Your mate outside isn't in on this, is he?" Electra was already suspicious.

Paul shook his head. "He doesn't even know I'm here. I've been doing some thinking and Barbados sounds sweet."

Electra smiled. "Good. You just missed Julian and the gang." For some reason, even though Rock was the only other one involved, she always thought of him as the gang.

"Will they be back?"

Electra nodded. "Yeah. Julian is dropping off my money around ten tonight. I think he's holding out on me. Probably on Rock too. That dim shit doesn't know left from right. You can stay here and follow him home. Then kill him at the door and call your cop buddies. Get the safe out the window, then say there was nothing."

"Are you sure this will work?"

Electra shrugged, not giving Paul much hope. "It'll work long enough to get us to Barbados, Paulie."

"What about Rick?"

She shrugged again. "I'll distract him. He's watching me after all. I can just walk off and he'll follow like a puppy. Then you can track Julian easily and nobody will notice either of you."

Paul nodded. "I sure as fuck hope this plays out as you think it will."

"It will, Paulie, it will."

They sat back and watched films and TV reruns as they waited for ten to arrive. This confirmed what Paul had been suspecting: that Electra was his dream girl, the ideal, who would be by his side forever. He was certain of it. It had to be fate. He held her close and counted his blessings. If there was justice in the world, he would pull off the killing and they would be able to live happily together somewhere where nobody would ever discover what they had done.

Soon Julian messaged Electra to say he was on his way. Electra kissed Paul and looked him in the eye as she promised him it would all work out. Paul was quickly bundled into the wardrobe as Electra questioned herself and her choice in men again. Was Paul really right for the job? Could she trust him? The idea was that she would get her money off Julian, see him off then rush out to distract Ricky as Paul followed Julian home. It seemed like a sensible plan to her, but she still had her questions. She hoped Paul could actually go through with it and finish Julian and hand the vault out the window. She hoped she could make it there after losing Ricky. She hoped Rock wouldn't still be there. She hoped nobody would suspect a thing. It was all very difficult. She calmed down by telling herself that, should it all go to waste, she could always just play the "vulnerable chick card" and try and get out of it by pushing the blame onto the men. A gang ringleader and a corrupt police officer fighting it out wouldn't exactly sound wrong to anyone. And she would be safe.

She greeted Julian and tried to keep her face looking as sour as possible as she accepted the money and shouted at him about the cut she'd got. She shouted at him about how she'd had to service and then kill the cashier to keep everything running smoothly. Julian slapped her, as she expected him to, and she went silent and said something about going out to buy cigarettes. She left and Julian slipped back out the window. There was nothing more she could do. She wandered towards the store, knowing Ricky was on her heel. There was no way he could suspect the people sneaking in and out the windows. There was no way he could guess that his coworker was in cahoots with her. The plan was flawless. All Paul had to do was fire a couple of shots and blame it on Julian, which would be easy as Julian was an armed bank robber with a house full of weed.

Paul saw it as less clear cut. This shooting would be a lot of paperwork in the very best case scenario. Electra was worth it for the trouble, but he was hoping for a very fast getaway. Especially after hearing that she was the killer. Of course, she could have been making noise, saying anything to get a rise out of Julian... but he suspected she wasn't. Electra was a killer. And he was about to become one as well.

He tracked the man all the way to a bungalow in a run-down neighborhood. The place was probably nice a while ago, but those days were long gone. Julian walked in and left the door ajar. Paul always understood that as a sign he had or was expecting company, but he couldn't be too sure. He crept up to the door and peered in. Coast clear.

But Julian was aware of the man on his trail. And he suspected that this man and Electra were working together. He had no idea of the rest of the plan, though. He did not know that Paul was a police officer. He did not know that Paul was armed. He did not know that Paul was not planning a robbery, but a killing. So Julian sat back and watched TV and waited for his would-be burglar to make an appearance. He knew he was there and he knew he could get him with a bat or a gun before he could try anything.

Paul wasn't sure what to make of it. He spied through the crack of the door and soon noticed something was amiss. Julian was too obvious. Too ready. He knew someone or something was coming and he was prepared. Paul wouldn't be able to dodge this one. Julian was ready for him. He just needed to ask himself exactly what Julian felt he was ready for. For a policeman? Possibly. For a murderer? Possibly. For a robber? Possibly. For all three? Almost certainly not.

Paul braced himself. This would be the only way to do it. He stood upright and pushed the door open, gun in hand, finger on the trigger.

As Julian leaped up and brandished his own weapon, Paul knew that was all it would take. He fired three shots into Julian's chest. And then the man was down in a pool of his own blood. He hadn't expected Paul to be armed or ready to kill. And it had cost him. Paul cautiously checked Julian's pulse. He was dead. Next, he investigated the room. At first he was hit by the worry that it wouldn't work out, that the money or the safe weren't there. But he found the safe eventually and pushed it out the back window, as Electra asked him to, before calling Ricky to ask for backup. He had found a suspect, been assaulted and had to fire shots. The man was dead and they would need to be there as soon as possible.

What Paul didn't know was that the plan hadn't gone as smoothly as he and Electra had planned. Ricky hadn't been the only person observing Electra's house. Paddy had been planted further down the street and, while he hadn't seen Julian's initial visit, he had definitely seen the second visit along with Paul's less than stealthy exit after Julian.

Paddy was a man to stick to his job above everything else. He may be a touch paranoid and the other officers mocked him mercilessly for it, but it was born of a strong survival instinct and almost pathological perfectionism. He always needed everything to go smoothly so he always expected the worst. Needless to say, he hadn't foreseen this at all. Not that Paul would betray them like that. Or run his own completely illicit investigation. Paul had always been as by the books as Paddy was. But this didn't disappoint Paddy. He couldn't be disappointed. He expected the worst of everyone. So he had calmly followed Paul to Julian's house and watched as Paul spied on Julian. He wanted to know what Paul would do next and he had little reason to call anyone yet. After all, if Paul could arrest Julian it would save everyone time and Paddy's faith in humanity would have been slightly restored.

But it wasn't to be. He heard Paul fire gunshots. Then silence. Concerned, Paddy sneaked up as close to the window as he could and tried to look in. Paul was moving something heavy right towards him, though fortunately not looking at the window at that particular moment. Paddy moved to the side just as a large safe landed by his feet. This was gold. Not literally, but it was gold. This was all he needed. Then, as he heard Paul leave the bungalow, Paddy got the radio message that Paul would need backup due to a surveillance plan gone wrong.

At first Paddy wasn't sure what to do. He was the closest officer. But would his closeness be suspect? What if Paul worked out what had happened? Then again, he had to know. Paddy couldn't be certain that Paul was acting selfishly. Maybe it was all with good reason.

Gathering his courage, Paddy reported to the front of the bungalow, where Paul waited. Paul didn't seem shocked at what was happening. Paddy radioed that everything was under control before turning to Paul.

"So... What exactly happened here?"

Paul was a little surprised that Paddy was there, but he wrote it off as that they were all hot on Julian's tail. "I was following this man, I thought he was Harry Julian, a suspect."

Paddy raised an eyebrow. "But you were off duty?"

Paul nodded. "A policeman is never off duty."

Paddy smiled. "And you managed to track him? How did you work out where he was?"

"I just figured it out."

"What if I were to tell you that I saw it all?" Paddy revealed. "Could you be more honest with me then?"

Paul had not anticipated this. Anything else he was prepared for, but not this. "You saw it all?"

Paddy nodded. "I'm sure your behavior can be explained. How you came to be in Electra's house, why you followed Harry Julian out the back."

But Paul couldn't explain it. He didn't think he would have to and he was at a loss. There would be no negotiating with Paddy, no making secret arrangements for a portion of the money. The best he could do

would be distract him until Electra had collected the money and then...
Then what? Paul knew what he had to do. He just didn't want to.
Killing a criminal in the line of work was one thing. But killing another
officer to cover up a crime? A crime he had committed for another
criminal, so they could both run away, nonetheless. He wasn't sure he
had it in him.

Paul wondered whether Electra could get away without him.
Probably not. She needed to be clear.

Electra was soon there and noticed the police officer in front of
Paul. She froze and watched them. Could Paul be trying to betray her?
But no, Paul was guiding the officer away. She wasn't sure she could
trust him any more. Why could she never trust the people she needed
to trust? But from the hill she could also see the safe that had been
pushed out the window. If there was any chance of getting it before
Rock got it, before the officers returned or before Ricky was back on
her tail, it was now.

Electra walked calmly down the street, keeping an eye on the car up
the road where Paul and the other, uniformed officer were talking. They
didn't look her way. She moved round the back of the building and
opened the safe. There was a lot more than the four hundred thousand
Julian had claimed he had. It was quite likely that was all there was,
that he'd made one and a half million like they had planned. It was also
possible that they'd made even more and Rock already had his share.
But Electra wasn't bothered. She moved the money into her shopping
bags and purse and calmly walked back the way she came. Nobody
would notice a thing.

Paddy hadn't noticed her. Paul had been watching the safe and was
very grateful when Electra appeared, emptied it, locked it again and
disappeared. There was one fear that remained in her mind: would she
do a runner with the money? Or did she love him, would she wait?

Someone else who had witnessed the incident was Rock. He had
been staying at a friend's flat across the road, looking down on the

whole row of bungalows. He had seen Julian being stalked, he had heard the shooting and he had seen Electra collect the money. But he wasn't too bothered. It served Julian right, for messing with a woman like that. He wanted out of it now. He'd spent too much time out in the open, committing crimes and staying away from honest work. He would use his money to buy himself a flat and learn a trade, take on an apprenticeship in IT or something equally promising. Then he could sell the flat and move somewhere in the country, work from home and own his strawberry field. It would all come together. He wasn't ready to get caught yet. He just had to lay low until it all blew over.

So he just leaned on the window sill, knowing the light reflecting off the glass was hiding him, sipping his beer and chatting to his friend about something and nothing, watching Electra walk away with the money as the cops bickered. Rock didn't get how both those cops had missed Electra. Surely one of them had seen her sneak round the back and empty the safe? But they were too busy arguing.

Then, through the glass, Rock faintly heard another shot fired. The uniformed officer fell to the ground. Rock raised an eyebrow but sighed. There was no point calling anyone or getting involved. It was too dangerous. He walked towards the kitchen and got himself another beer.

Paul didn't know how he had managed it. One moment he and Paddy were arguing about the situation and Paul's apparent over involvement. The next, Paul had shot Paddy in the gut and the head. It wasn't instinct. But he didn't even remember pulling out the gun, removing the safety and pulling the trigger. Paddy hadn't expected it at all. He hadn't even taken out his own gun. He just lay there, a crumpled form, like he had fallen asleep in an awkward position.

Paul didn't know what to do. He had killed a policeman and backup would soon follow. The only thing he could think of was to move the body. It would be discovered, but it could buy them some time to escape. This was a pretty bad area. Shootings were common, killings were common. Nobody would question another police officer's body, some extra shots or a car.

Clumsily, Paul heaved Paddy's body into the car. There was little blood underneath him, so it probably wouldn't be noticed. The best way of getting rid of it would be to drive him somewhere else. But that would be too suspicious. Instead, Paul looked down the hill. It was still quite steep. The car should roll back fast. Leaning in, he pulled the hand break and watched the car roll off before he made his way back to Electra's flat.

Electra was there, counting her money. Ricky's car had been nowhere to be seen, although after the incident with Paddy, Paul couldn't be too sure any more. Electra, despite the fact she had just had her ex boyfriend killed and probably knew about Paddy, was bubbly and happy. She didn't care about these deaths, about these crimes. Three people's blood was on her hands, but it didn't particularly bother her. She was just happy it was going so smoothly, that she was getting the money.

"We did it, Paul. We have a cool million and a half now. All ours. We can go to Barbados and buy a nice house on the beach."

Paul nodded.

Electra sensed he wasn't all that happy with the arrangement any more, but that didn't matter. He wasn't going to betray her. Worst case scenario, she could leave him here to get caught. "Did you get rid of the other officer?"

Paul nodded again. "Yes. Paddy's gone, but we're going to have to get moving soon."

Electra raised an eyebrow. She wasn't quite sure what Paul meant.

"You can't kill a policeman at a crime scene when people know where you are. It means they will find you. They know your flat and they know me. We need to go."

Electra sighed and stood up, stretching so her back cracked. "I guess so. You go get your shit and find us a motel. Here's some cash.

When you have it, come and collect me in the morning. Then we can book our flight and fuck off to Barbados."

"Do you even have a passport?"

Electra nodded. "I've been planning on getting away from Julian for a while now. Anyhow, you need to get home, get your shit together and get to a motel. They know you were there, but nobody knows I was involved here and I want it to stay that way."

Paul nodded back. "I get you. See you tomorrow."

"See you tomorrow." Electra kissed him deeply, a hint of what was to come for the rest of his life. Almost all his worries, concerns and anger faded away. He would do anything for Electra. He would kill, rob and skip the country to Barbados. She was worth it all.

As Paul left her flat, he made sure nobody was watching it. Rick still wasn't back and there was no sign of anyone else. They were probably busy at the crime scene. He needed to get his things before anyone suspected him or went to his house. Which would be soon. He waved at Electra's neighbor as he walked past and she smiled and waved back before going inside.

As he suspected, his flat was not under surveillance, but he had a few missed calls on both his mobile and his landline. Then he worked out what was happening. He had been there and killed Julian in the line of duty. Paddy had joined him. Paddy's body was down the road, bleeding out into his crashed car. And there was blood all over the bungalow and the street. They suspected Paul had been killed or kidnapped. Thinking fast, Paul tried to not make his flat look much different. He grabbed some money but left his wallet. He grabbed a couple of forms of ID but left his birth certificate. He took some very old clothes and some food and threw it all into an old bag before escaping.

He locked the door and put on a hooded coat. Then, he took a taxi to the highway and stopped at the first motel. Everything was perfect. His car wouldn't move. His body wouldn't be found. He could leave a note on Electra's door saying she had ran away and that she and some thugs had kidnapped him to make themselves safe. It would buy them even more time. He texted her the details and she agreed it sounded good.

If he was a hostage then nobody would suspect anything. They could get away safely and nothing would interfere. Paul went to sleep feeling comfortable in the knowledge that they were getting away to Barbados in a matter of days.

Ricky arrived at Paul Sanchez's door and found it locked, just as Paul would have left it. They had already worked out someone had used Paul's gun to kill Paddy and were fearful for Paul's life and safety. But the girl, Electra, had simply returned home from shopping and there was no sign she had been anywhere near there. Besides that, no woman her size would have so easily lifted the safe and hauled it out the window. Perhaps the thugs that followed Harry Julian and his gang had finally come back for what they wanted, what they felt they deserved. They money had been gone. Whoever came for it either knew the combination to the safe or was sorely disappointed.

Ricky had managed to get permission to investigate Paul's flat. He broke down the door and found it empty. Everything was as Paul would have left it: a complete mess. Food in the fridge, his wallet on the side. That should have calmed any suspicions Ricky had. But it didn't. Because Paul's car keys were on the side, his driver's license was missing and his voice mail had been accessed. Of course, it could all be innocent. But Ricky suspected that someone had been there. Someone who shouldn't have been. Maybe a criminal, maybe Paul himself. And they didn't want anyone to understand what was happening. They knew how to hide such matters from the police. But they didn't know how to hide Paul's nature from his long-time coworker.

When Ricky got back to headquarters he found Kenty was a little behind on the news. Kenty was still following an old lead that Julian had been sighted near the flat. Paddy's old lead. Of course, the information was useful: Julian had visited Electra. But it wasn't grounds for anything yet. They needed a search warrant to get into her house and they were pretty sure they wouldn't get one.

Ricky updated Kenty on the deaths: Julian, Paddy and possibly Paul. Kenty shook his head. "Two fine young officers." Ricky hadn't the heart to suggest what he suspected. After all, chances were he was over analyzing anyway. How likely was it that Paul had anything to do with it? More likely was that they dragged him home and took his passport so they could hop the border with him. Maybe he left his keys as a sort of sign that Ricky would be able to follow. All that was more likely than Paul being somehow involved.

That night, Kenty released a press bulletin explaining that a few people had died and a valuable officer was still missing. He urged anyone with any information whatsoever to come forward as soon as possible.

Paul was asleep in his motel room bed already. Dreaming about waking up in silk sheets with Electra wrapped around his body and the sea lapping the wall around their house during high tide.

Electra was sat up, smoking and drinking and packing her bags, trying to keep it to two cases although one was full of money, hidden by clothes and cookware. She didn't watch the news and wasn't in the mood for TV anyway, as her paranoia was setting in.

Rock didn't own a television and was sat up drinking beer on his own at his own place, having just returned from his friend's house. He was pondering how to stay out of the police's way until it all blew over.

But Ann saw the bulletin. She wasn't a dedicated watcher of the news, but she enjoyed having some sound in the background as she went about her chores. She had been an earnest worker since early childhood, when her mother had died and her father took over caring for the six children. He would bring home the money and she would clean and cook and make sure everyone was ready for school every day. Despite the odds they had done very well and Ann worked only mornings at a local office, leaving her plenty of time to garden, cook and socialize. But she would still stay up late to finish her chores, do the laundry and maybe read a book. And as she was ironing her shirts for the next day she had the news on in the background.

The bulletin didn't mean much to her. She knew there had been a robbery a while back and that earlier in the afternoon they had found the ringleader's body. And good riddance too. She wasn't glad of his death, but she was glad he had been found. The news that there were more gang members, some armed thugs that had rebelled against their leader and kidnapped a policeman, made her shake her head. She was an old soul and couldn't help but feel that in times gone by these things just didn't happen.

But she did remember seeing the police officer somewhere before, the missing man. Of course, he had been wandering the street a few days ago, possibly on the hunt for any criminal activity going on in the flats opposite. She knew the woman who lived there in the second floor was a drug dealer and that the ground floor was home to some prostitutes. So she wasn't surprised that a police officer would be round there. But no, that wasn't quite it. She couldn't remember, but she had seen him somewhere and she seriously couldn't remember where.

As she lay in bed, thoughts danced in front of her eyes. But she didn't put them together until the next morning.

Paul made his way to Electra's house under the cover of dawn. The taxi pulled up outside, but even though she had replied to his text by saying she was getting up, she was nowhere to be seen. He texted her again and she still didn't reply. He asked the cabbie to wait for them and went upstairs to hammer her door down. He had heard on the radio on the drive down that the police were asking people to come forward and seeking warrants for various houses, which probably included Electra's. They needed to get her out of there and leave the note on the door.

Paul had scribbled a ransom note on the motel paper and was planning on sticking it to the door to be found by Ricky. Electra had not, as she had told him, been getting up and was still nude. However much he wanted to ravish her then and there, he explained the situation and Electra got dressed quickly. But not quickly enough. As they taped the note to the door and darted downstairs, Paul realized the cab had driven away, probably not desiring to stay in a slightly bad area more than a few minutes. He knew he shouldn't have paid the man in advance. Paul's belongings were still at the motel, so that much was safe, but they had to call another taxi and wait on the curb.

As Ann walked around the house opening the upstairs windows before she went to work, she spied Paul and Electra out of the corner of her eye.

The night before she had vaguely remembered his face, but now there was no mistaking it. Electra's handsome visitor was the missing policeman. Ann didn't know the ins and outs of the situation. And she didn't want to meddle with another person's private matters. But she also didn't want to not report Paul to the police. Stood by her window, she called them and explained what she saw.

Ricky, on the other end of the line, put two and two together. Even though he and Kenty had been up all night seeking a warrant, they raced to their car and asked Ann to wait inside until they arrived. The situation might be about to become dangerous.

Ann was happy to oblige, but after ten minutes Paul and Electra were still there. The police and the taxi were both stuck in the awful morning traffic and Ann was starting to worry about getting to work late. She grabbed her bag, put on her shoes and headed out the door. She smiled and waved at Paul and Electra as she got into her car and checked her bag to make sure she had everything.

It all happened at once. The police arrived before the taxi did. Paul spied them and grabbed Electra, who grabbed her bag of money. They darted towards Ann's car. Ann couldn't bring herself to start it or run into them. In a matter of seconds, Paul, Electra and the bag were in the back behind her and Paul was pressing a gun to the back of her head.

"Drive. Highway. Now."

Ann nodded. She felt frozen, but she knew what she had to do. Somehow keeping her cool, she started the car and made her way towards the motorway.

Paul didn't know what he was doing any more. Someone had got a search warrant for the house or someone had tipped off the police and now they were after him. They had seen him and Electra patiently waiting for their taxi on the curbside. They had seen him take a hostage. It was too late. They were in too deep. He needed to evade the police, get the bag from the motel and make his way to to the airport where he and Electra could slip away. It would be fast and then it would be over.

When they got to the motel, Paul grabbed Ann by the neck as he exited the vehicle, then pointing the gun through the window and asking her to get out. "I'm sorry." He apologized. "I don't want to hurt you. I just need to use you as... well, as a shield, so we can get away."

Ann shook her head, holding back tears. "Please don't do this. I have an elderly father to care for. I'm still young."

"I won't hurt you." Paul was getting more and more nervous. This had escalated far beyond what he was happy to work with. This was far too dangerous, far too much. He guided Ann into the motel, with Electra staying behind, a gun in her own hands, guarding her money with her life. Paul was in too deep now. He had killed a criminal and a police officer. He had betrayed the force and kidnapped an innocent woman. And he was on his way to Barbados with his dream girl.

His life couldn't be fixed here any more. He could only try and get away as fast as possible. He locked the door and made Ann sit on the bed as he checked he had everything. She was still almost crying. But he didn't know what else to do.

Everything was in the bag. Now all he had to do was... Ann's eyes were locked on the motel room window. Paul looked up. Ricky stood there, gun in hand. Without thinking, Paul took aim at Ricky. Ricky braced himself and fired two shots.

Paul felt a burning pain spread down his arm and through his chest. He had been hit through the lung and in the shoulder. He dropped the gun and collapsed. He wanted to be afraid of dying. He wanted to avoid it. But the fear was gone. He had thrown everything away. He pulled himself to his feet. Ann ran to the window, but he made no move to stop her. She was blocking Ricky's gun from delivering a fatal bullet.

Maybe there was still time? Maybe there was still a chance?

He staggered outside. Kenty stood outside, several officers around the car. Electra was standing beside it, gun in hand, scowling. She still wanted to get away. She knew she couldn't, but she was furious at how she had been set up, how she had been caught. She couldn't pretend it was all the guys now. It had gone too far. They knew.

She spied Paul staggering out of the main entrance and ran over to him, dropping her gun. It was all over. They weren't going to Barbados. They weren't keeping the money. No little house in the sun or handsome pool boys or busy shopping sprees in richly scented markets.

Paul collapsed over her shoulder as the policemen drew closer. His arm wrapped around her shoulder as he kissed her, his wounds pressing blood into her arm, shoulder and breast.

"Tell me..." He sighed. "Tell me, baby. Could we have had a chance without the money?"

He collapsed before she could answer. He was dead.

***

Rock walked around his new flat and looked out the window onto the garden. It was a nice place. He was glad it had come up for sale after Electra had gone to prison and her rent had expired. He wouldn't have wanted to rent it, after all. But owning it wasn't bad and with how inexpensive it was he could always rent it out once he moved and make a small income that way.

He, like everyone else, had heard about the case from the news in bars and the odd newspaper or magazine he'd read. He was surprised, but not shocked at how it had all come together. He had done well to lay low. Over the course of the few months in hiding he had carefully paid his money into his account, claiming to be a male escort. Nobody would try and trace a John for proof that he, or in his case she, had hired a prostitute. The plan had worked flawlessly and Rock was pretty impressed with himself. By eight months he had enough money to finish paying for the flat and move in. He would continue claiming he was a male escort until he had no more money to deposit.

The next move was less calculated. He couldn't force her, after all. But they had something in common and he hoped to bond over that. Despite everything she had been through, Ann was staying in her ground-floor flat opposite, still going upstairs to care for her elderly father in his flat, still working hard. Rock was impressed at her toughness and had used his old connection with Julian to flirt with her. She hadn't been shocked or scared and agreed to go on a few dates with him. They had already been to the cinema and he was planning on taking her to a fancy Greek restaurant the next evening. She "knew" he was an escort and didn't mind.

She was lovely. Pretty, non judgmental, hard working, a loving daughter and tough as nails. She was the sort of woman he wanted on his strawberry farm.

Rock waved at her out the window as she worked on her flower beds. He smiled lightly, a rare smile, as she blew him a kiss.

END